"Why have you come to me?" Kit asked, his gaze never leaving hers. He took another step toward her.

"Stop!" Kristine pleaded. But he kept moving closer to her, and the question in his eyes demanded an answer. "We need to work," she said.

"As you wish." He touched her face with both hands and brushed her hair behind her ears. He cupped her face in his palms. She didn't run when he grazed her cheek with his mouth. Instead, her eyes drifted closed and her knees weakened. She didn't run when his caress roamed down the side of her nose to her mouth. Her lips parted, waiting for his kiss, and she wondered at the magic of his touch.

His heat enveloped her in a cocoon of masculine scents, tantalizing her with a promise he didn't fulfill. His mouth hovered above hers, and he touched her only with the softness of his breath and the palpable desire she sensed flowing off him and into her.

The wait was maddening. Her body pleaded with her to move, to close the spare inch separating them. She licked her lips and felt the barest touch of his mouth on the tip of her tongue, the almost imperceptible tightening of his hands on her face. He was that close, but not taking her, and she was unraveling inside.

He wasn't an outlaw, but an enchanter; not a monk, but a shaman skilled in the art of seduction. Without even a kiss he had her aroused, panting, melting inside. . . .

WHAT ARE *LOVESWEPT* ROMANCES?

They are stories of true romance and touching emotion. We believe those two very important ingredients are constants in our highly sensual and very believable stories in the *LOVESWEPT* line. Our goal is to give you, the reader, stories of consistently high quality that may sometimes make you laugh, sometimes make you cry, but are always fresh and creative and contain many delightful surprises within their pages.

Most romance fans read an enormous number of books. Those they truly love, they keep. Others may be traded with friends and soon forgotten. We hope that each *LOVESWEPT* romance will be a treasure—a "keeper." We will always try to publish

LOVE STORIES YOU'LL NEVER FORGET
BY AUTHORS YOU'LL ALWAYS REMEMBER

The Editors

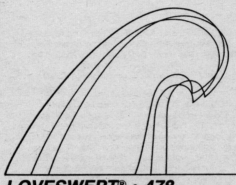

LOVESWEPT® • 478
Glenna McReynolds
Outlaw Carson

![logo] **BANTAM BOOKS**
NEW YORK • TORONTO • LONDON • SYDNEY • AUCKLAND

For my friend, Sandy. Thanks
for all the laughter
we've shared.

OUTLAW CARSON

A Bantam Book / June 1991

*If you would be interested in receiving protective vinyl
covers for your Loveswept books, please write to this address
for information:*

*Loveswept
Bantam Books
P.O. Box 985
Hicksville, NY 11802*

ISBN 0-553-44097-7

Published simultaneously in the United States and Canada

*Bantam Books are published by Bantam Books, a division
of Bantam Doubleday Dell Publishing Group, Inc. Its trademark, consisting of the words "Bantam Books" and the
portrayal of a rooster, is Registered in U.S. Patent and
Trademark Office and in other countries. Marca Registrada.
Bantam Books, 666 Fifth Avenue, New York, New York
10103.*

One

"I can't work with the man," Kristine Richards announced. She tossed the memo from the dean of the university onto the piles of clutter on her desk, starting a small avalanche of papers.

Jenny, her elderly graduate assistant, crouched down and retrieved a few of the letters, stuffing them into her arms, already filled with many other important papers.

"Won't, not can't," Jenny said, looking around for someplace to stash the unattended-to business. No empty space magically appeared. Sighing in resignation, Jenny opted for the last resort, collating the correspondence by using the thousand or so books lining the walls of the office. She made sure an edge of each envelope stuck out from the volumes. Within a minute, the shelves looked like they might take off and fly.

"Okay, have it your way," Kristine agreed easily. "I won't work with the man."

"The university is already into Carson's Tibetan project up to their ears," Jenny said, "and they want to make sure the findings get published. You're the logical choice for his assistant."

"Then they should have made darn sure I was the one chosen to go to Tibet in the first place. But no, they sent Harry Fratz, and Harry caught some god-awful bug. Lucky for Harry."

Less than a year ago, Kristine had been stunned and thrilled to learn that her employer, Colorado State University, had been selected to help fund—and then share in the glory—of an ambitious archaeological study. A renegade archaeologist named Carson planned to compile an inventory of ancient Tibetan monasteries, temples, and shrines. Kristine had been certain she'd be picked to go along as Carson's assistant. No one on the university's staff was more qualified, least of all Harry—except by virtue of his gender. But they'd picked Harry, who had barely lasted two months, and now the whole expedition was in shambles, an international disaster.

They had a lot of nerve, she fumed, trying to drag her in on the tail end of Carson's Catastrophe, as the history department now labeled the project. The whole damn thing should have been Richard's Reward from the start. She knew more about Tibet, fact and fiction, than Harry had ever even bothered to imagine.

She sorted through the junk on her desk, finally coming up with a chocolate chip cookie. She blew a little dust off one edge and took a tentative bite.

"You're going to die someday," Jenny admonished her.

"I'll be in good company. What else does the

university have to offer their finest Asian historian for summer employment, besides sorting out somebody else's mess and babysitting the glory boy who made it?"

"Probably a pink slip."

Kristine choked on her cookie. Jenny patted her on the back.

"There, there, honey. I hear the community college is looking for a history teacher."

Kristine raised her watery eyes to meet Jenny's. She didn't doubt her assistant's summation of the situation. The older woman's uncanny intuition had never failed her when it came to the inner workings of the university.

"That's . . . blackmail," she gasped, reaching for her cold cup of coffee.

"You'll be dead before you're thirty," Jenny said as she watched Kristine use a pencil to stir the sugar up from the bottom.

Kristine swallowed a sip or two anyway. "Still in good company."

"But you'll probably live through the summer," Jenny went on. "It's up to you whether you do it working on Kit Carson's Tibetan findings or job hunting."

"Blackmail," Kristine muttered. Carson, she thought. Kit Carson. Even his name rankled her. What kind of fool name was Kit Carson?

A famous fool's name, she silently admitted. He'd come out of the vastness of Asia nearly ten years ago, dazzling museum directors from Beijing to Calcutta with the extent of his knowledge and the rarity of his archaeological finds. He was a virtual unknown who'd made a name for himself by being part of the spectacular excavation of the burial tomb at Lishan in China, with its amazing collection of thousands of lifesize terra-cotta warriors; a renegade Buddhist monk with unparalleled access to the secrets of the Far East.

She'd never met him. No one she knew had, except for poor, dumb Harry, and the hospital wasn't allowing visitors. Still, you couldn't get three historians in the same room without his name coming up, usually on the end of "That damn barbarian." It took only two archaeologists to reach the same consensus, both of them praying Carson wouldn't be the first to be allowed to excavate any of Tibet's hallowed ground. Tibet was an archaeologist's dream, but no one could do more than list any artifacts that were visible. It was illegal to dig at any of Tibet's religious sites.

Carson was too unorthodox to fit in the realm of academia, and he'd lost his reputation shortly after he'd gotten it. He didn't have a degree in anything, not even the equivalent of high school, if the rumors were correct. And if what they were hearing from China was true, while supposedly cataloguing Tibet's shrines and temples, Kit Carson had crossed the final line into out-and-out grave robbing.

Kristine groaned and dropped her head on the desk. The university must be desperate to threaten her with dismissal. Any tenured professor would refuse to work with Carson on the grounds of protecting his or her reputation, now that Carson had slipped into infamy. Unfortunately Kristine didn't have tenure or a reputation. "Publish or perish" went the old adage, and she'd be damned if she perished this close to a full professorship.

"Kristine, dear?"

"Yes?" she replied without lifting her head.

"That green rag you're wearing today is really too awful for words. I've told you a hundred times you're a winter."

"Thank you, Jenny," she muttered into the papers cushioning her face. Carson. Kit Carson. She groaned again.

The first two trunks arrived at her house the first Monday after finals. The second pair came on Tuesday. By Wednesday, Kristine and the delivery-man were on a first-name basis. The university, through Dr. Timnath, the head of her department, had insisted she accept Kit Carson's luggage, assuring her she'd need the trunks for her research and requesting that she be discreet. She'd countered with a mention of tenure, priding herself on being able to *discreetly* work it into the conversation three times. She was beginning to wonder, though, if the owner of the luggage was ever going to make a personal appearance, and whether or not she dared break off the heavy iron padlocks to see what was inside the fascinating old cases. One look at them had convinced her, albeit belatedly, of the wisdom of taking on the Carson project. Who knew what treasures lurked in the trunks' cavernous depths?

"Now, Bob," she said, Wednesday morning, yawning and scrawling her name across three of the tiny lines on his delivery sheet. Her second signature missed the lines completely. With her free hand she tightened her grip on the one hundred and twenty pounds of pure ugly she called a dog and most people called a beast. "I want you to notice I'm giving you an extra signature here. If you show up tomorrow morning, please put the trunks on the deck without knocking or ringing the bell. Okay?"

"It's against the rules, Kristine," the deliveryman said nervously, keeping one eye on her mastiff.

"Come on, Bob. Live dangerously. Bend the rules." And let her have at least one morning of sloth, she prayed. Last night there had been a welcome home party for Harry to celebrate his hospital release. She'd stayed much too late in a vain attempt to corner the guest of honor. He'd looked far healthier than she would have guessed for a man newly risen from his deathbed, and he'd avoided her like the plague.

"Okay," Bob finally said. "I'll try it . . . once."

"You're a great guy." She flashed him a smile, using the last of her strength.

Half an hour, two aspirin, and one mug of coffee later, Kristine draped herself over the open refrigerator door and searched for something edible. Mancos nudged her legs, whining.

"Yeah, yeah, I know. Old Mother Hubbard better get something for the cupboard."

The whining stopped abruptly, and Mancos whirled around, almost knocking her over in the process. He barreled out of the kitchen hell-bent for leather, sliding on the wood floor and letting out a woof that made coffee redundant.

Eyes painfully wide, Kristine shuddered and shook her head, trying to get rid of the ringing in her ears. She heard Mancos hit the dog-door at full speed, followed in the next second by a loud, deep, "Aaiieey-yah!"

"Dammit, Bob," she muttered, slamming the

refrigerator door shut and stumbling after the mastiff. She ran through the living room, threw back the curtains, and jerked the atrium door open—to the most amazing sight.

He was fast, she had to give him that, and light of foot, like a highwire artist. And he definitely wasn't Bob. He was racing along the deck railing, keeping either one step in front of or one step behind Mancos's snapping jaws. The morning light spilling over the foothills cast him in a golden halo, a color shades paler than the thick, silky hair pulled away from his face and hanging in a roan braid down his back. Shorter strands of dark auburn hair feathered across his cheeks and melded into the winged curves of his brows.

The sleeves of his black tunic were rolled up, revealing dark skin, tightly corded muscle, and more gold bracelets than she could count. A wide leather belt hung low on his hips, banded on one side with the hilt and sheath of a large, wickedly curved *khukri*, the blade of a Gurkha mercenary. His jeans were tucked into roughly made short boots, nothing more than flaps of leather sewn together with strips of rawhide that were secured with silver hoops at the top. He was a running wind chime, and the music of his quick steps left her stunned.

She really needed to do something to save him, she thought, or her dog, if he went for his knife. Then he saw her, and his flashing grin and sly wink made her instantly aware of a need to save herself.

She stepped backward with a hand to her chest, a blatant gesture of self-defense, and a totally inappropriate action for a contemporary woman living in an age when the only raiding hordes inhabited Wall Street. But the uncivilized look of him conjured up undeniable visions of a long-ago time, when women were women and men were the barbarians who took them.

Barbarian . . . Between one breath and the next she placed him, that damn barbarian, Kit Carson.

"*kukur, ahA!*" he shouted in a deep voice, watching the dog, but tossing her the chamois bag slung over his shoulder. When Mancos went for the bag, he clapped his hands and shouted again, recapturing the mastiff's attention. "Hey, dog!"

Kristine caught the heavy bag and clutched it closely, not daring to take her eyes off Carson or the animal so determined to eat him for breakfast. He wasn't afraid of the slavering, growling beast. The realization went through her with absolute certainty and wavering disbelief. Mancos's looks alone kept most visitors in their cars, honking their horns. But then he wasn't most men. He was the outlaw Carson, and she'd bet anything he was no Buddhist monk. Not with that smile.

The dog lunged for his ankle, and Kristine's fingers tightened around the strap of the bag. The melange of soft textures drew her gaze—the strap was made of silk and the finest leather, and a yard-long auburn braid that matched the color of his hair. Her jaw slackened as she raised her head to stare at him again.

He was pacing the rail now, not running, and Mancos matched him step for step, back and forth across the deck. He was talking to the dog, and the singsong lilt underlying the rough timbre of his voice mingled with the fresh, light sound of his bracelets, mesmerizing the dog and her both. When he hunkered down on the rail, she felt sure Mancos would snap out of it, but he didn't. Neither did she. The man reached down to scratch behind one of the dog's rusty-brown ears, and she almost dropped his bag in shock. Then, with seemingly no effort, he stepped off the rail. He didn't jump or leap. He just stepped, an act of power and grace that told her more about the muscles in his legs than any amount of running on the narrow rail. And he wasn't even breathing hard.

She wasn't breathing, period.

"*Namaste,*" he greeted her. Bracelets, beaten gold and chased in ancient designs, jangled as he touched his palms together. "Good morning."

"Hi," she said, but it came out more like the breath she'd lost than a word. Six feet of masculine brawn towered over her, gentled only by the teasing light in his eyes. The sheer size of him was overwhelming, and it was compounded by the energy she felt radiating off him. Renegade, outlaw, or monk, the man had presence in spades.

Kit grinned at the stunned woman. Finally, he mused, the long journey seemed worthwhile. He'd tracked his trunks across the breadth of America, from one fleeting destination to the next, until they'd led him here, to a house and a woman. His fainthearted partners had more than compensated for their irresponsible treatment of the trunks.

He took in her dishabille and the amazement in her eyes, and his smile broadened. If she'd been less beautiful, he would have been too tired. A wild cloud of dark curls tumbled past her shoulders, framing a face of untold delicacy; eyes of a color he'd never imagined, like mountain violets, and the palest skin he'd ever seen, skin delightfully unmarred by the heavy makeup that covered the faces of so many Western women.

"Concubine?" he asked, running his finger along her cheek. She was so soft, so beautiful, so welcome, he sighed. Yes, Shepherd and Stein had done well. He graciously forgave them for their cowardice and merely doubled the price of the treasures he'd risked his life to bring them.

Con . . . cu . . . bine, concu-bine, con-cubine. Kristine tried to untangle the word from his accent. When she did, her face flamed, especially where he'd touched her.

"No," she gasped, then put more force into the word. "No. I am not a concubine."

"Not mine?" One eyebrow lifted over spice-colored eyes, spice like cinnamon, dark, rich, and mysterious.

"No. No. Not yours."

"Too bad, eh?" His grin flashed again, more dangerous than before.

Yes. The word formed in her mind, and she chased it out on rapidly beating wings of panic. "I am . . ." She took a deep breath and tried again. "I am Kristine, Kristine Richards."

"Kreestine, Kreestine?" he repeated, smiling again to ease her discomfort. Kristine felt anything but eased by the inherently sensuous curve of his mouth and the glimpse of strong, white teeth. Sensuality, she'd learned the hard way, was a thing to be avoided at all costs.

"No, just one Kristine," she explained when she found her voice again.

"Ah, Kreestine," He rolled her name off his

tongue, putting a lilt on the second syllable. "Very pretty."

"It's a—a nice enough name," she stammered, wondering when her brain was going to kick back in.

"No." He slowly shook his head and his grin faded. Capturing her chin with a large, rough hand, he tilted her head back, immobilizing her with the gentleness of his touch and the light in his eyes. "Kreestine is pretty," he murmured, his mouth lowering to hers, his breath warming her lips.

A flood of heat poured down her body at the slight touch. When he sealed his mouth over hers, her last shred of sanity followed. She melted as a masterfully strong arm wrapped around her waist and pulled her close, close enough to feel every curve of muscle in his chest and the tautness of his abdomen; close enough to feel the rising tide of his desire and his iron-hard thighs.

Good Lord, she thought through a haze of faintness. His tongue asked for and gained purchase into the recesses of her mouth. He tasted sweet, musky sweet, like honey from a faraway land, and he kissed with an abandon to match the wild flavor, completely, exotically.

Ravished. The indescrible feeling spread through her mind as the moment slipped deeper into fantasy, further from reality. She was being ravished and she really needed to stop it before she decided she liked it.

More than beautiful, more than tantalizing, Kit discovered so much in her kiss. His first instant of astonishment slowly transformed into curiosity, then into exploration. With the patience of the ages he began to learn the pleasure she gave. He followed the path dawning in his mind as he deepened the kiss, drawing her ever closer, the way he was being drawn.

Ah, she should have been a concubine, he thought, but even as a simple keeper of his hearth she was more pleasing than any other. He'd been right to come to this unseen land of his mother and father. He'd been no monk. No amount of beating had changed the truth that the life of aesthetic riches had not been for him. He'd been meant to live this life with all its joys and pain.

Drawing on her strength for what she knew was her one and only chance, Kristine pushed against his chest. Where was Mancos when she needed him?

"Aaiieyah," he whispered softly into her mouth, helping her push away.

She looked up dazedly at the pained expression on his face. Goodness sakes! Had she hurt him?

Hurt him? What was she thinking? She should have slapped his face.

"The dog likes you better than me?" he asked.

She followed his gaze down the length of his body to where Mancos's huge jaws were wrapped around a mouthful of jeans and undoubtably the leg beneath. No sound emanated from the jowly animal, a good sign.

"M-Mancos, shoo, shoo." She flicked the tail end of her robe at him, grateful for the distraction and the chance to catch her breath. What in the world had she been thinking, to sink against him like some sunstruck coed?

"Sha, sha?" she heard him repeat above her head.

"Shoo . . . uu," she instinctively corrected him, then wondered if she'd lost her mind.

"Sha-sha, Mancos. Sha-sha." He raised his foot and shook it the slightest bit. "Sha-sha." The dog did, but only a little. The ugliest head on the continent lifted just far enough to shove into the man's crotch. He laughed, a deep, rolling sound that seemed to wash all through Kristine. And then he embarrassed her beyond the ends of the earth. "Not for you, Mancos." He pushed the dog away. "For Kreestine."

She figured her only glimmer of hope lay in the heretofore unheard of possibility of spontaneous disappearance. Of course, it didn't happen. Her luck hadn't been running in the right direction for miracles lately.

Or had it? Her own laughter rose in her throat, but she couldn't tell if it was a mature response to his or the beginnings of hysteria. He took the opportunity to steal a kiss off her cheek, his head bending close to hers, his braid sliding over his shoulder. She knew it was hysteria she fought.

"*Namaste*, Kreestine," he murmured.

"*N-namaste* . . ." She knew who he was, knew the only person he could be, but she still didn't believe it.

"Kautilya Carson," he said, filling in the blank left by her trailing voice.

"Kit Carson?" she questioned breathlessly, having never heard the other name.

"Westerners say Keet, yes."

"The Buddhist monk?" she asked, attempting to clear up one of the obviously more doubtful rumors she'd heard about him.

"No. I am not a monk." He laughed and touched

her cheek again, as if she needed reminding of the kiss they'd shared. "I ran away before they gelded me."

"They geld the monks?" She hadn't read anything about gelding in her comparative religion textbooks.

"They try, in the mind," he explained. "But some like boys."

And she certainly hadn't read that in any textbook.

"Don't worry." He laughed again. "They didn't get me. You taste like coffee. Do you have coffee?"

She absolutely did not believe this. She didn't believe any of it. He tasted of honey, and she tasted like coffee. They'd barely met and all they'd talked about and attempted was sex, an occurrence so rare in her life and so far back in her past, she'd completely forgotten what all the fuss was about until he'd reminded her. Oh brother, had he reminded her. She needed to go back to bed and give the morning another shot at normalcy.

"Yes," she blurted out in panic, realizing bed was the last place she dared to go. "Yes, I have coffee."

"Good." He reached for the bag dangling from her hand and slung it over his shoulder. "Let's share coffee."

In the five feet stretching from where she'd stood on the deck to the front door, she managed to stumble over thin air.

"Careful, Kreestine." He laughed and reached out to steady her. The warmth of his hand only flustered her more. "Did you hurt yourself?"

"No. No, I'm not hurt." She really needed to stop repeating herself, she thought. Then she ran into something substantially harder than thin air.

"My fault."

He grinned, and that, she knew, was something he really needed to stop doing, if she was going to get her pulse slowed to a reasonable pace. He bent down and picked up a huge duffel bag, slung it over his shoulder, then hefted a large trunk onto his other shoulder, a trunk to match the six already piled in her living room.

If she hadn't seen it with her own eyes, she wouldn't have believed it. Even with a ton of luggage weighing him down, he moved with more grace than she could have imagined, as if his feet weren't touching the ground.

Two

"I think you've made a mistake," Kristine said. And as soon as she cleared it up and sent him on his way, the better, she added silently. Which didn't begin to explain why she was pouring him a cup of coffee. He stood on the opposite side of the breakfast counter, not close, but not far enough away to suit her. Not when she could still feel the warmth of his kiss, and not when she was still in her it's-seen-better-days bathrobe.

"Mistake?" he repeated.

"Yes, a mistake." The cup rattled on the saucer as she picked it up. His hand immediately steadied hers, but also sent her pulse racing. She stared at the calloused fingers covering hers on the rim of the saucer. Prominent veins laced the back of his hand like a river delta, a confluence of life flowing beneath richly tanned skin.

"I've made many mistakes in my life, Kreestine. Could you be more specific?"

16

His admission surprised her, but no more than the man himself. She wasn't exactly sure what she had expected, but even in her wildest dreams she wouldn't have imagined him. Who would have?

Asian sensibilities overlaid a face and body of pure European extraction, and the soft mysteries she'd seen in his eyes defied his Caucasian heritage. He wore his hair long, like a Khampa warrior, but the color told a different story, a story of Scottish highlands and fair-skinned people. Despite the muscular grace of his movements, despite the natural ease with which he wore his foreign trappings, the man didn't fit together. She couldn't think of a single series of events that would have placed him in an Asian monastery, let alone brought him out into the world on the wings of sudden renown.

She lifted her gaze to meet his, a definite mistake. He was color and energy, tangible, fascinating energy. Thick lashes shadowed his spice-hazel eyes and the smudges of weariness beneath his mahogany skin. His nose was straight, chiseled by a divine hand to match the planes of his cheekbones, the clean lines of his face, and the rugged strength of his jaw dusted with a day's growth of dark beard.

The unchecked wanderings of her mind surprised her, and she realized she'd been staring at him for much too long, somehow having gotten lost in all those mysteries in his eyes. She cleared her throat and broke the spell-like trance. "I'm not sure who sent you here," she said, "but they must have told you who I was, Kristine Richards?"

"No one sent me," he said with a grin. He dropped a handful of sugar cubes into his cup, more sugar than even she would have attempted to get into a single serving of coffee.

He must have misunderstood, so she tried again. "You didn't talk to Harry Fratz or somebody from the university?" she asked helpfully, hoping to jog his memory and trying to ignore the jump in her pulse every time he smiled his roguish smile. She unconsciously shook her head to negate her unnerving response to him, the shiver winding its way down her spine.

He cocked one brow in confusion, his eyes narrowing. "You know Harry Fratz?"

"Yes," she said, overcoming a ridiculous urge to run, trying to be the helpful hostess.

"Ah, then I have made a mistake," he said with another sly grin. "Harry doesn't have the imagination to think of a concubine."

"I should hope not!" she exclaimed, shocked out of her politeness and her wayward thoughts. "Harry and I are associates, professional associates." Concubine, indeed!

"You aren't my housekeeper?" He tilted his head to one side, sending his braid sliding across the black cotton and one broad shoulder. Rather than detract from his masculinity, his long hair added an extraordinary touch to what was arguably the most male animal she'd ever met. Everything about him spoke of eons long past, every rough edge, every mannerism—except his eyes, for what she saw there was timelessness itself.

She took a deep, calming breath before replying with all the propriety she could muster. "No, Mr. Carson." She paused for a second, aware of how inappropriate the title sounded. Mister implied a degree of civilization she doubted he'd attained. "I am not *your* housekeeper. I am Kristine Richards, Dr. Richards, Harry Fratz's replacement, which you would have known if you had bothered to check in with the univers—" A light bulb clicked on in her head like a floodlamp, giving her another pause. When she continued, she did so with a gaze much narrowed by skepticism. "And if you didn't talk to anybody at the university, how did you know to come here?"

"I followed the trunks." He gestured behind him to where the trunks lay stacked across her living room floor in all their curious splendor.

As explanations went, his was sorely lacking in salient points. She lived a good five miles outside of Fort Collins, up in the foothills of the Rockies, and most people couldn't find her house with a map full of directions. Correction, she thought. No one could find her house *without* a map full of directions.

"You followed the trunks," she repeated, allowing every single one of her doubts show.

His innocent yet oddly ancient gaze held hers. "Things of power always leave a trail. It is your choice whether or not to believe."

Things of power, she repeated silently. *Right.* She shifted uneasily, casting a wary glance at the trunks. She'd thought they were plenty strange and plenty old, what with their heavy iron hinges and padlocks, the oiled leather reinforcements on the corners, and the intricate grid of metal holding the blocked planks together, but she hadn't felt any power coming off them. In truth, she was damn glad she hadn't.

"Do you have cream?" he asked.

"Uh, sure," she stammered, dragging her gaze

away from the trunks. His fingers brushed hers again as she handed him the carton of cream from the refrigerator, physically reminding her of the energy he embodied. *Things of power.*

Dammit-all, she thought. Somebody should have warned her about Kit Carson. Harry was a milk-sop, but surely Dr. Chambers, the dean, or Dr. Timnath, her department head, had known more than they'd told her. The list of digs and articles she and Jenny had compiled on Carson didn't begin to add up to the enigmatic man standing in her kitchen, looking for all the world like he'd just ridden into a caravanserai somewhere on the Eur-asian steppes.

Plastering a wan smile on her mouth, she backed away from the counter. She spied a box of choco-late covered doughnuts, and shoved them in his direction. "Have a doughnut, please. I'll be back in a moment."

She didn't exactly flee into her office, but neither did she dawdle on the short trip across the living room.

Kit leaned on the counter and helped himself to a doughnut, watching Kristine until she disap-peared, enjoying the quick sway of her hips be-neath the white cotton robe and the determined set of her shoulders. She wasn't what he'd ex-pected or initially hoped for, but she would do. She would more than do.

For fair measure, he tripled the price of his treasures. Shepherd and Stein had failed on all counts, especially in the destination of his trunks. Harry Fratz, frightened fool that he was, had made the university's position on contraband quite clear. They didn't want anything to do with his more questionable activities, no matter how nobly motivated. His partners should have accepted the trunks he'd shipped from Nepal and trusted him to obtain the documentation necessary to soothe their collective legal conscience. His unorthodox means of delivering the Tibetan antiquities had obviously scared them off, but he'd thought Shepherd at least was made of sterner stuff. He'd thought her convictions were strong enough to weather a small storm of Chinese anger and empty threats. He'd been wrong, and she'd unloaded the trunks on this unsuspecting university professor.

He didn't bother to waste anger on any of them. He'd known the probable outcome of his last mission long before he'd crossed the border into Tibet. The Turk, the damnedest brigand of the plateau, wanted a second chance to sink his knife into his heart; the Chinese had posted his name and face at every guard station; and the Nepalis had kicked him out of the land of his birth. He could not go back, not legally, not yet.

He'd weighed the risks and found them worth taking, and only regretted that Kristine Richards hadn't had the same opportunity. But due to her ignorance in accepting the trunks his partners and the university had sent her way, or Shepherd's and Stein's cowardice, or even the winds of Fate, she'd become his responsibility. What he'd felt in her kiss made him lean heavily toward Fate. He'd spent too many years of his youth under the yoke of Buddhist monks to mistrust his instincts, and his instincts were still mildly and pleasantly aroused. He'd been too long without a woman not to enjoy this one in whatever capacity she allowed.

All in all, he had no complaints with the turn of events and no doubts about his ability to protect Kristine until his business was finished. Maybe he would quadruple the price—for the price was his to set—and give her a portion of the rewards. She had surely taken on part of the risks.

Picking up another doughnut, he pushed away from the counter and strode over to his trunks. He knelt by each one and methodically checked the padlocks, holding the doughnut between his teeth. The heavy locks were secure. She hadn't given him reason to question her honesty, but the trunks had passed through many hands before falling into hers.

He bit off a hunk of the sweet and ran a gentle hand over one of the trunks, smiling slightly as he chewed. He had found the legendary monastery Chatren-Ma, and the *Kāh-gyur*—the Buddhist scripture—of the last great khan, Kublai. His smile broadened into a grin. Or at least he'd found as much of it as had been in the monastery, about one-fifth of one volume of the whole one-hundred-volume set. Still, it was more than anyone else had ever been able to get their hands on, and it guaranteed him a full belly for as long as his days in this life lasted.

In her office, Kristine hung onto the phone, listening intently to the muffled voices on the other end of the line. She'd started at the bottom of her list with Harry, but her eavesdropping didn't bode well.

"Dr. Richards?" Harry's wife came back on the line. "I'm sorry, but Harry has had a bit of a relapse and is unable to take calls this morning. "

Relapse, my foot, Kristine thought. "I'm sorry to

hear that," she said sweetly, tapping her pencil on her desktop. "He looked so healthy last night."

"Yes, well, I think the party was too much for him. I'm sure he'll call you when he feels better."

Don't bet on it, Mrs. Milksop. "Be sure and tell him his old friend Kit Carson has finally arrived. I'm sure he'll want to see Harry while he's in town."

"I . . . uh, don't think that's a good idea. The doctors are afraid Harry might be contagious or . . . uh, something. Good-bye."

The phone clicked in Kristine's ear. She pulled the receiver away and gave it a good long look, her free hand sliding the pencil through her fingers. Harry's wife was either a terrible liar, or half the history department at Colorado State University was in for a very rough summer. If Kristine believed for a minute that Harry was contagious, her next call would be to buy shares in Poudre Valley Hospital.

Instead she called Dr. Timnath, who was conveniently out of town. Convenient for him, not for Kristine.

That left Dean Chambers, the man who held her tenure bid in the palm of his hand. She'd been kowtowing to him for nine solid months and really hated to ruin a perfect streak of subservience with an irate phone call. Maybe if she forewent the irate part she'd be okay. The man would surely want to know his outlaw had come home to roost—on her doorstep.

Thinking only pleasant thoughts, Kristine punched in the dean's number with the chewed eraser end of the pencil.

"Hello," the man himself answered on the third ring. There was no mistaking the deep bass of his voice. It was one of his greatest tools of intimidation.

"Good morning, Dr. Chambers. This is Kristine Richards."

"Yes?"

So much for idle pleasantries, she thought. "I'm calling to tell you Kit Carson has arrived, and I was wondering . . . uh, wondering what you wanted me to do with him"

"*Do* with him, Dr. Richards?"

She rolled her eyes heavenward. On the downswing she got waylaid by the sight in her living room. Outlaw or not, Kit Carson couldn't possibly be doing what she thought he was doing. She craned her head to the right and watched in growing disbelief as he rolled something up in a cigarette paper and licked the edge.

"Dr. Richards?" Dean Chambers's voice rumbled into her ear.

"Yes," she hissed into the phone. "*Do* with him. He's—" She stopped abruptly, lifting her head and sniffing the air. Tobacco. She immediately calmed down. Then she got riled all over again, watching wide-eyed as he blew smoke rings into her pristine mountain air. Perfect smoke rings, one after the other, sending little ones through big ones, single ones through double ones. The smoke hovered above him, holding shape in concentric circles long after it should have dissipated. She'd never seen the like.

". . . suggest you work with him," she caught Dean Chambers saying. "You have Harry's preliminary research. If you had doubts about your qualifications for this opportunity, you should have spoken up before agreeing to the project."

She snapped her attention back to the phone. "No, that's not it," she said quickly. "I'm more than qualified to write up Carson's findings, but—" But what, Kristine? But he kissed you? Right, that was just what Dr. Chambers needed to hear. "But he's . . . but I'm . . . but he doesn't . . ."

"Is there a problem, Dr. Richards?" The dean's voice cut through her confusion like a knife.

"He's strange," she said weakly, knowing how stupid it sounded. At least she had enough presence of mind not to add that he was better looking and more of a barbarian than the dean could imagine. She'd always thought that derogatory term referred to Carson's methods, not his personality. His kiss had wiped that little theory right out of her mind.

"He's apparently led a strange life," Dr. Chambers said. "If he's having trouble adjusting to his new environment, I suggest you act as his cultural liaison. Your efforts won't go unrewarded."

The words "things of power" were on the tip of her tongue, right on the very tip, begging to be released. She fought the urge with everything she had inside her. Concentrating on those elusive rewards, she tried to get the conversation back to something that would highlight her intelligence.

"Have you made arrangements for his accommodations?" she asked. "He seems at loose ends." Not brilliant, she thought, but not stupid.

"I'll leave that up to you as his cultural liaison. Frankly, from what we've been hearing these last couple of months, we weren't at all sure Mr. Carson would fulfill his contract. You might contact faculty housing." The dean paused, and Kristine heard a disturbing hesitation in his voice when he continued. "Remember, Dr. Richards. We are only interested in Mr. Carson's provisional inventory of the ancient remains of Tibet. I recommend you concentrate your efforts on the research we paid for and not on whatever else he may be involved in. He is a man of many talents, not all of which we wish to be associated with."

Perfect, she thought. Absolutely perfect. "You've been very helpful, Dr. Chambers," she said, refraining from sarcasm. "Thank you." She hung up the phone in disgust and plopped her chin into her hands, knowing she'd just been royally dumped on.

His cigarette finished, Kit walked over to a window that looked out over rolling hills leading to a reservoir, the escarpment beyond, and the city on the plains below. The redwood deck swept around the north and east sides of the house. The south side was a glassed-in area with a quarry-tile floor, filled with plants and sunshine. Her house was so open, far different from his own in the upper reaches of the Kai Gandaki River in Nepal, near the Tibetan border. His house, which he had lived in for several years, had been built to hold off the cold of bitter winters and the winds funneling down through the gorge. Hers welcomed the elements into every room. He would enjoy the comforts it offered.

The comforts and the company, he thought, discounting the small lack of an invitation. His partners had obviously not seen fit either to send an explanation with the trunks, or to make any arrangements for his arrival. In all likelihood, they probably hadn't thought he'd get out of Tibet alive, not with the Turk battling for the prize he'd attained. But the woman had a doctorate, and he'd sensed even greater intelligence than the title implied. She would surely respond to reason, and if not, he'd learned much of the art of persuasion from his second father, Sang Phala.

Still in her office, Kristine waited for yet one more telephone transfer, knowing her options were dwindling faster than the snow in the high country. Faculty housing was booked until Saturday, the married students housing had a waiting list two pages long, and the dorms were full for the next two weeks with the Christian Crusaders.

The secretary came back on the line. "Dr. Richards?"

"Yes?"

"I've found a cancellation in Corbett Hall, but—"

"We'll take it," Kristine blurted out.

"But it isn't a private room," the secretary finished.

"That's his problem," Kristine muttered under her breath, and thirty seconds later had given the secretary all the information she had, his name and a billing address to the history department.

With her first success of the day under her belt, she went out to garner another one, getting rid of the most intriguing man she'd met in many a moon. The irony wasn't lost on her.

"We're in luck," she said, gaining his attention as she entered the living room.

"I have felt the same," he replied, turning with his rogue's smile in place. His eyes darkened with the same warmth she felt in his smile, chasing the lightness out of her heart.

She girded herself against the intensity of his

gaze by tightening the sash on her robe. It was far too early in the morning to be thinking the thoughts racing around in her mind, and he was far too much of a stranger to have put them there.

But he hadn't felt like a stranger when he'd kissed her, and there weren't enough hours in the day for her to explain that discrepancy.

"I meant, I've found you a place to stay. The university will pick up the tab, but"—she unwittingly shook her head to match the movement of his, and her words slowed—"I'm afraid you'll have a roommate—" She suddenly realized what she was doing and stopped. "Is there a problem?"

"I must stay here, Kreestine," he said, his gesture taking in the whole house. Her house.

"Here? Right here?" Surely she'd misunderstood. There seemed to be an awful lot of that going around.

He nodded, and she found herself again following along, her hair brushing against her shoulders. With effort, she jerked her head in the opposite direction.

"No. No, I don't think so." She shook her head vigorously. "You can't possibly stay here. It's totally out of the question. Impossible."

"Imperative," he countered.

"Unreasonable," she said more firmly.

"Ordained."

"Ordained?"

"You have accepted responsibility for the trunks. In return I must accept responsibility for your safety. There is no other way."

Kristine stared at him, dumbfounded. Her first instinct was to call Dean Chambers back and reexplain the situation a little more succinctly. Or better yet, demand he talk to Kit Carson himself and get a good dose of what she'd been up against all morning. The man needed more than a cultural liaison. He needed a full-blown course in Western civilization. One in logic wouldn't hurt either.

"Good, we are agreed," Kit said, taking her silence for the necessary acquiescence, pleased he hadn't had to resort to more energy-consuming means. The journey had been very long, tiring his mind as well as his body. "I will need food and rest. Then we will begin sorting through photographs and my accompanying notes. We lost a mule in a river crossing, and one of the yaks disappeared into a crevasse, but these things happened early in the journey, and I'm sure they were only carrying supplies and not journals. Still, the inventory must be checked. Our camp was raided under the shadow of Mount Tise, but once again the gods were with us and the bandits did not get what they had come for, though one of the muleteers was injured. Sometimes, this is the way, is it not?"

His wild story caught at her imagination, despite a strong warning that told her to cut short his litany of disasters and insist that he leave—before her curiosity completely overruled her common sense. But the longer he talked, the more curious she became, especially about healthy Harry.

"When did Dr. Fratz jump ship?" she asked baldly, playing a disturbing hunch. "After the mule, or did he make it through the raid?"

Kit chuckled and shook his head. "Ah, Harry. He has no heart for adventure, no heart at all. He abandoned the caravan shortly after we crossed the border into Tibet, which was just as well. It was his mule we lost."

"He wasn't sick?"

"Only with fear."

Her hand tightened into an unconscious victory fist. She'd suspected it the night before, and now she knew. That milksop had run out on an expedition she would have given her eyeteeth to be on, river crossings, disappearing yaks, bandits, and all. Now, instead of sharing in the glory of discovery, she'd been relegated to sorting and writing—neither of which required a bodyguard, as Carson had implied.

She glanced back up at him, silently admitting he would make an impressive one, if one was needed. Which it was not, she firmly reminded herself. The very idea was ludicrous. No woman needed a man for protection, or anything else as far as Kristine could tell. She'd gotten along quite well without one for four years. Actually, she'd gotten along better without one. She had no intention of ruining the winning combination of herself and her work by allowing some overly charismatic outlaw to breathe down her neck while she resurrected his project from the shambles a bunch of men had made of it.

Drawing in a deep breath, she prepared to explain her position in formal tones befitting their professional relationship. "I'm afraid you'll have to make do with a dormitory room for a couple of days, Mr. Carson." There was that title again, appropriate for the circumstances, but oh so inappropriate for the man himself. "On Saturday you can move into one of the faculty apartments. It is completely outside the realm of my responsibility or the confines of custom for me to allow you to stay in my home. I hope you understand." And she did, fervently. She didn't know what she'd do if he didn't. Calling the police seemed rash, and unlikely to forward her career.

"Then we are not agreed?" he asked, looking surprised. It was a rare emotion for him, if she was reading his underlying reaction correctly.

"No, we are not agreed."

"I thought you understood about . . ."

"And I wish you would understand," she said over his uncompleted sentence.

Forbearing a sigh, Kit lowered his gaze and dragged a hand through his hair. Sang Phala had taught him many things, but the old lama had obviously never dealt with an American woman. He wondered if they were all so self-determined, or if it was a purely personal trait in Kristine. He was used to women who obeyed without question and had little knowledge of women who didn't. It was an interesting experience, interesting and a shade irritating.

Kristine crossed her arms over her chest and watched him carefully, trying to gauge how he was taking her ultimatum. He didn't look angry, but he didn't look like he'd given up either. For the life of her she couldn't imagine why he was insisting on staying. Sure, she'd responded to his kiss with unprecedented enthusiasm, but her every action since had been designed to discourage him. If her ex-fiancé had shown even half of his tenacity, she might be married now instead of heading into spinsterhood with only her degrees to keep her warm.

Maybe she should try another tack and stretch her authority a bit. The man might be more infamous than famous at the moment, but he was still a visiting scholar of sorts.

"If you would prefer a hotel," she said, "I'm sure the university will pay for your room and board." They were already into his project to the tune of thousands and thousands of dollars. What was a few hundred more? "We have a number of fine establishments here in Fort Collins, including a bed and breakfast place close to the school, The Charters House. The Mountain Inn has a swimming pool and it's just a couple of blocks from my office, or there's the . . ."

So be it, Kit thought, only half listening as she extolled the virtues of all the places he would not be staying. He'd never found any protection in innocence or ignorance, though at one time he'd had both in abundance. He didn't want to frighten her, but she'd left him no choice.

"Kreestine," he interrupted, and waited until he had her undivided attention, until her mountain-violet eyes focused on him, impatient but waiting. "Others will find the trail harder to follow, but one will come, and before he finds me, he will find you. I cannot leave until it is known that what I have brought is no longer within his reach."

A brick wall, Kristine thought. It was like talking to an inscrutable brick wall. "Who will be coming for what?" she asked in exasperation, pressing him to make a point, any point at all, without beating around the bush.

Kit started to tell her the details were unimportant, then hesitated, caught by the spark of warning in her eyes. Not just the pertinent facts, he decided, but the truth with all its unknowns, with all its possibilities.

"The Turk will come for the treasures of Chatren-Ma," he said. He spoke the last word softly, like the invocation it was, and the immediate change in her eyes told him she knew exactly what the name implied.

Kristine opened her mouth to speak, but no words formed on her lips. The man had an unsurpassed ability to stun her into gaping silence, but he'd definitely made his point.

She finally found the wherewithal to choke out a word. "Impossible."

"Difficult and dangerous, but not impossible," he said. "Not for me, and not for the Turk. He led the bandit raid on our camp. An ocean will not stop him."

Absolutely impossible, Kristine insisted silently. The professor in her refused to believe in the fabled monastery lost in the clouds and snows of the high Himalayas. She'd sooner believe in Atlantis or Shangri-la. She knew the famous legend of Chatren-Ma. It was supposedly the resting place of the earthly remains of the lama of Saskya and the *Kāh-gyur* he'd translated into Mongolian for Kublai Khan, the Mongol conqueror of China in the thirteenth century. As a historian specializing in the Trans-Himalayan region of Asia, which stretched with the Himalaya Mountains from Afghanistan through India, encompassing countries such as Nepal and Tibet, she'd read a lot of legends. Tibet, in particular, was awash in them. The forbidden land grew legends and gods and demons

with abandon, and few scholars had ever penetrated its veil of mystery.

And now here was Kit Carson, Kautilya, as big a
mystery as any she'd read about, speaking of
Chatren-Ma and bandits. Of course, bandits.

Three

Every archaeological site in the world was seething with bandits these days, Kristine knew. Especially if the site was fabled, as most were before they were "officially" discovered by someone with an academic title. That didn't do an archaeologist in Tibet any good, because everything in Tibet was too sacred to excavate. Hence Carson's provisional inventory of *visible* historical remains, a parameter he'd obviously always intended to push to the limits and beyond. No wonder Harry had turned tail, she mused.

"Was the monastery intact?" she couldn't resist asking, then felt foolish. How could a nonexistent monastery be intact? But then maybe, just maybe, sometime in the night the stars had aligned in a manner to sanction miracles. *Chatren-Ma!*

"Will you give me a week to conduct my business?" he asked, ignoring her question.

She ignored his, forcing her voice into calmness. He seemed so sure. "Can you prove it?"

Thrust and parry, Kit thought, allowing a half smile to form on his mouth. He hadn't wanted to frighten her and he obviously hadn't. Why hadn't the university sent him this woman in the beginning? Taking Harry Fratz back to the Nepalese border had cost him two days he could have used to stay ahead of the Turk. Then again, if the school had known about his true mission, they wouldn't have sent anybody. He'd needed their nominal inclusion to convince the Chinese of his more honorable intentions.

Kristine watched him slip a long chain with a key on it from around his neck. He strode over to the trunks, his boots jingling in muted tones, his long legs powerful and sure of their destination. Despite the necessity for skepticism, her excitement flickered, then stirred into vigorous life.

He opened one trunk, then another, and another, easing the lids back to expose not the treasures within, which appeared to be nothing more than layers of ivory-colored fabric, but the trunks themselves. The inside panels were black as the night, and made up of wooden blocks, long, narrow rectangles worn smooth at the edges. Into each block was carved, with intricate delicacy, rows and rows of script. Kristine's hand slowly lifted to cover her mouth, and she took a step forward. Strips of leather nested between the blocks, protecting them, and were interspersed with tufts of the ivory fabric flecked with black.

"My God," she whispered, moving closer. She reached out with her hand but didn't touch. Inches away, her fingers curled into her palm. The cloth was more than mere fabric. He'd packed the trunks with prayer flags, cushioning the ancient printing blocks with layers of holy invocations to the gods.

"They'll have to be studied," she murmured, "put in the labs, dated and analyzed. My God." She eased closer yet and peered inside one of the lids, forcing herself still not to touch. She tilted her head far to one side, studying the printing blocks. "It looks Mongolian, but it's hard to tell backward, and I'm no expert."

"But I am, Kreestine. My partners know this and will pay dearly for the opportunity to own what I have brought. They will run their own tests."

She whirled back around, the words "grave robber" flashing across her mind. "You can't sell them!"

"Of course, I must sell them. I cannot protect them indefinitely. Already I have risked my life and the lives of many others to bring Kublai's *Kāh-gyur* out of Asia."

The *Kāh-gyur* of Kublai Khan, she thought, hidden through the centuries in the monastery of Chatren-Ma. Suddenly too many things made sense: the rumors coming out of Asia, the way he'd shown up unannounced and unaccompanied, the university's slapdash coercion, Dr. Chambers's final warning, Harry's reclusiveness. Everything made sense except her stupidity in buying it all at face value. She'd always considered herself heavy on the intelligent side of the brains or beauty equation, until this morning.

"I cannot condone the theft of a priceless historical relic, the heritage of the Tibetan people," she said staunchly. It took more courage than she'd thought she had to confront him, this strange barbarian from the frozen wastelands of "the roof of the world." Historians didn't take a Hippocratic oath when they received their degrees, but there were some lines she couldn't cross. He stood on the other side of them. "I should call the police."

"I have been outrunning the authorities for a month, Kreestine," he said softly. "Now would be an inopportune moment for them to catch up with me."

His statement caused her pulse to race and her face to flush. What had she gotten herself into? "You should have thought of that before you stole the *Kāh-gyur*."

"I did not steal anything. Your university is not the only institution concerned about the survival of Tibetan history and archaeological sites. The Tibetans themselves have a much greater stake in salvaging their heritage. They contacted me, and I promised to do what I could."

"The Tibetan government?" she asked, only slightly reassured.

"The exiled Tibetan government. Do you understand?"

Yes, she understood. She knew the Chinese, who had invaded Tibet in 1950 and forced the Dalai Lama, the spiritual and political leader of Tibet, into exile in 1959, were tearing up sacred ground as quickly as they found something they considered of value—like uranium, or gold, or a religious rallying point for an oppressed people.

The outlaw Carson, she mused. He'd been well named. Where else would an outlawed government go for help except to another outlaw? Who else but an outlaw would have dared such an expedition? And who else but Kit Carson would have apparently succeeded?

She didn't buy his "things of power" routine, at

least not completely. She'd done enough investigative research of her own, though, to know that when people wanted something badly enough, they usually found it. Luggage that had traveled halfway around the world, especially trunks as notably unique as his, would leave a paper trail a mile long, and it was her signature scrawled across Bob's clipboard three days in a row. Carson had certainly found her.

She had two choices, she figured. She could sue the university for negligent, reckless endangerment of her bodily person; or she could drop down on her knees and thank the Lord and Harry Fratz for giving her such a golden opportunity. If Carson was lying, she was smart enough to distance herself from the hoax before it reached damaging proportions. That was a chance the university and Harry obviously had been unwilling to take, especially considering Carson's means of acquiring the *Kāh-gyur*. If he spoke the truth, and if she could pull it off, she'd have Dean Chambers eating out of her hand. For the barest instant she imagined herself in a circle of glory, turning down offers from Yale, Harvard, Stanford, holding out for Cambridge or Oxford.

Calm down, Kristine, she told herself. Think this thing through. But excitement and rampant curiosity were clouding her judgment. She recognized the double-whammy from lifelong experience, and from having given in to them both more times than she cared to admit. She'd agreed to marry Dr. John Garraty, her mentor at the University of Colorado, in a buzz of excitement, and that decision had turned into an unmitigated disaster that continued to haunt her life like a proverbial bad penny.

But Chatren-Ma . . . Now there was a prize worth bending the rules for. She had the world to gain and nothing to lose but her common sense and a little sleep while Carson stayed in her home.

Kit felt her wavering, and he felt the surprising strength of her ambition pushing her in his favor. It was all he needed to dare a slight trespass. Yet even as he reached out to caress her brow, he wondered about this new depth to the woman he'd mistaken for a concubine and a housekeeper. Courage was admirable in both, but intelligence and ambition were dangerous in the former. He'd have to watch her carefully, not only to save her from the Turk if he managed to find them, but to save her from herself if the need arose.

He touched her in silence, letting go of his troubled thoughts for the moment necessary to insure the invitation she was allowing and he had to insist upon.

Say yes, Kreestine. You will have no regrets, and I am too tired to argue endlessly over what has already been decided.

Kristine stepped back, wondering what in the world had compelled him to touch her again, and wondering why in the world she'd enjoyed the brief contact. She covered her embarrassment by saying the first thing that popped into her head. "You must be tired."

"Yes, Kreestine." He laughed softly. "I am tired."

For better or worse, she knew what she had to do. Ten minutes ago she'd been racking her brain, trying to figure out a way to get rid of him. Now she wasn't going to let him out of her sight until she'd gotten what she wanted, a future in which she called all the shots.

"Well, you can't stay here," she said, "In the house, I mean. But there's a room above the garage, and you're welcome to use it until you. . . . until you dispose of what you've brought." She hesitated again. Hardball negotiations weren't her forte, but she was determined to make something out of her damnable luck. "I want—"

He silenced her with the slight tracing of his finger along her chin. "For your safety and my pleasure, I will meet your condition. My only wish is to place the *Kāh-gyur*. I will give you my knowledge of Chatren-ma." He touched his palms together and bowed his head in a gesture of compliance. "You may seek your destiny as you will with the gift."

Either the man was damned intuitive, Kristine thought, or he'd read her mind, which was, of course, ridiculous. She slanted a cautious glance in his direction. Ridiculous, she assured herself. No one could read a mind she'd obviously lost.

"Well, you just march right back out there and tell him to leave!" Jenny exclaimed over the phone. "Goodness sakes, Kristine, I can't believe you invited the man to stay up there in the woods with you!"

"It's not the woods, Jenny," Kristine said, tucking the portable phone between her shoulder and her ear as she dug through her sock drawer in search of a matched pair. "And I already have a mother. What I need is a friend who can—"

"And I should call her right now and tell her

what her crazy daughter has done. Muriel won't like this, young lady. She won't like this at all."

"Well, I'm not about to tell her, and if you don't, she'll never know." Many times over the past year Kristine had doubted her decision to take on as her assistant the oldest graduate student in the history of the history department. None of the other professors had to put up with being called "young lady" by their assistants, or have their nutritional knowledge challenged at every turn. But Jenny had proven her worth more than once, especially when it came to the minutiae of research and office politics. "Besides, Jenny, you were behind this project one hundred percent."

"I thought it would be a good career move for you to work with the man. I didn't expect you to take up with him!"

"I haven't taken up with him." Pink, white, blue, striped, hearts, argyles, cotton, nylon, wool. How could a person have so many socks without two of them even remotely resembling each other? Kristine wondered, digging deeper. "I need you, Jenny, bustling around the office for a week, looking busy. I'm giving you free rein. Organize whatever you want, throw out the rest." She picked up a purple sock and, miracle of miracles, found another.

"You're up to something, Kristine Richards, and I want to know what it is. Every time I get near that trash can you pitch a fit."

"So take advantage of my temporary insanity."

"Tell me, Kristy," the older woman insisted.

Kristine sat down on the edge of the bed to pull her socks on, then immediately jumped back up. Searching in the pile of sheets and blankets she found a long-lost hairbrush and stuffed it into the pocket of her robe. "I'm just doing what you told me to do, Jenny. I'm making a career move, working my way up the ladder."

"Kristine." Jenny spoke her name slowly, with the voice of authority granted her by her years. "I know the man has an international reputation, but it's not all that good, and there is absolutely no way for you to sleep your way to the top in this business."

"You've shocked me, Jenny, really shocked me." She tugged one sock on and reached for the other. "You know I don't sleep with anybody for any reason." The instant the words were out of her mouth, she knew she shouldn't have opened the discussion.

"And you're not getting any younger," Jenny shot back. "It's time for you to get back into circulation. Muriel and I still don't understand why you stopped seeing Grant Thorp."

"I wasn't seeing him. We had three dates, three long, boring dates, and I wish you and my mother wouldn't talk about me behind my back. Can we get back to business."

"We could if I knew what business we were talking about."

"Suffice to say, Carson doesn't want the trunks moved, and he doesn't want to leave them. Therefore, he stays here with the trunks. Simple logic." She refrained from using the word protection, knowing it would only unnerve her·assistant. "All I'm asking you to do is field any questions that might come up for the next week. Nobody seems to want anything to do with him, so you shouldn't have too much trouble."

"Nobody except you," Jenny said knowingly. "What does he look like?"

"You wouldn't believe me if I told you." She switched the phone to her other ear as she shrugged out of her robe and hung it on a hook. A moment later it slid to the floor, but by then her hands were full with juggling the phone and trying to pull on her jeans.

"Try me," Jenny said.

"Well, he's got this auburn braid hanging down to his shoulder blades and—"

"Red?" Jenny interrupted.

"No. Darker, more chestnutty. When he stands in the sun you can see the red highlights, but in the shadows or inside the house it's mostly dark brown."

"Hmm. What color are his eyes?"

Kristine snapped her jeans and thought for a moment, staring off into space. "Cinnamon. Just like cinnamon, and really soft, and really old."

"Hmm-mmm."

"And he's got these gold bracelets, a couple of pounds of them." She broke contact with the phone for a moment to pull a black sweatshirt over her head. "I think they're Scythian, if you can believe it."

"I see," the older woman said in a clipped tone.

"So what do you think, Jenny? Will you cover for me for a week?"

"I will if you'll make darn sure you cover yourself. Is Mancos there?"

"Alive and drooling."

"Good. I'll call you if anybody on this end decides to forego their reputation long enough to take an interest in Fratz's Folly."

Kristine sat back down on the bed and reached for a tennis shoe. "The last I heard it was Richard's Ramble Through the Ruins."

"Well, yes," Jenny admitted, then added, "The bets are running five to one against you coming up with anything publishable by the end of the summer. Half the department doesn't think Carson is going to show up at all. He's never left Asia before."

"He did this time," Kristine said.

"And the other half doesn't think he did the job he was funded to do."

"I've got seven trunks full of journals and photographs and—and other things that say otherwise." She was glad Jenny couldn't see her grin. "Don't worry. Come September, you might be working for the head of the department."

No idle boast, Kristine realized ten minutes later as she prowled through the one trunk he'd allowed her access to. This one was made of plain wood and held only legal research, no forbidden treasure. The man's documentation was meticulous. Notes and photographs were collated and color-coded, dated, numbered, and inventoried into a master list with a backup file, and his knowledge was astounding. He'd made inferences and conclusions she would never have dreamed of making. A quarter of a way through a preliminary review of his journals, she stopped long enough to call Jenny back. He'd practically written the book himself.

"I'll meet any bet dollar for dollar, double for Harry," she said.

"He's in for twenty," Jenny said.

"Then he's out for forty, that spineless wimp."

Hours later, Kristine was still entering Carson's

master file into her computer, double-checking each serial number and description with its corresponding photograph. A lock of hair fell over her face, and she anchored it back into her untidy bun with a bobby pin. She had finger-combed the tangled array onto the top of her head, having somehow misplaced her hairbrush for the second day in a row.

"Wonderful," she murmured around the pencil clenched between her teeth, as she held a photograph under the light of her desk lamp. She may have been crazy to let him stay—the longer she thought about it, the less concern she had for his bandit theories—but the project itself was everything she'd dreamed it could be. And this was without the extra tantalizing prize he'd offered. She had to write up the legal findings first, that went without saying, but afterward she was going to set Asian history and Dr. John Garraty on their heels.

She picked up her coffee mug and slumped back into her chair, almost laughing out loud. Yes, Dr. Garraty was in for a surprise. She dropped her reading glasses on the desk and slowly swiveled her chair around, changing her view from one wall of bookcases to another wall of bookcases, then past the glass doors leading to the deck and overlooking the city, then right smack dab into Kit Carson.

She pressed her toes into the floor, abruptly halting her swiveling. A splash of coffee soaked into her sweatshirt, and she hastily brushed at the stain.

He'd showered, shaved, and changed his clothes, and she was in no way prepared for the sight of him in his jeans and a T-shirt. The long shirtlike garment he'd worn earlier had hidden much of what she'd felt when he'd held her close. Without it, she had to come to grips with a lean, muscled body, dark-skinned arms, narrow hips, and broad shoulders outlined by pure white cotton.

"*Namaste*, Kreestine." He smiled as he tied off his braid with a strip of chamois leather.

The house wasn't big enough for both of them, she thought. Not with his way of filling up a room by barely stepping into it, and not when she felt surrounded by him when he was a good ten feet away.

"*Namaste* . . . Kit." She spoke his name for the first time and felt another barrier crumble, one she quickly tried to reconstruct. "You must be hungry. I made you some dinner. Why don't we go into the kitchen." At least it was a much bigger room than the one they were squeezed into at the moment.

She pushed out of the chair and rounded the desk, silently willing him to move out of the doorway before she got there, and almost wishing he *could* read her mind.

"I hope you're not a vegetarian," she went on. "I'm a little low in the fruits and vegetables department right now. I usually do my shopping on Thursday and today is Wednesday, so I'll go tomorrow." She rambled on, but he hadn't moved an inch. "If you need something special, I'll be happy to—"

His warm hand wrapped around her upper arm, stopping her in her tracks and jarring her pulse into overdrive.

"I'm not a vegetarian." His gaze roamed over her face, without once meeting her eyes.

"Well, good," she said. "Then you won't mind—" What was he doing? "Won't mind—" She raised her hand to stop him as he raised his own hand to her hair.

She's done the most amazing thing to her hair, Kit thought. He admired the sheer force of will it must have taken to tame the wild mane, but it wouldn't do. He pulled a bobby pin free.

"Do you mind?" she gasped, picking the pin from his hand and trying to push it in as he took out another one. In the heat of all her buzzing excitement, she'd conveniently forgotten the more personal effect he had on her, as well as the less than professional moments of their initial meeting. He'd just reminded her of both in no uncertain terms.

"Mind?" Kit repeated. A lustrous, dark tumble of hair slipped free, and he smiled. The woman was exquisite, delicate of face and body, and softly rounded in all the right places. He'd like very much to see her in a silk the color of her eyes.

"Yes, mind," she said. "You can't go around ruining people's hairdos." A few more tendrils fell free over her forehead. She was losing the battle, inside and out.

"Hairdos?"

"My bun," she said, tight-lipped. The man *was* a barbarian. She raised both her hands to salvage the mess and found there was nothing left to stick a pin into. He was fast, too fast.

"Ugly bun," he said, eyes sparkling with mischief. "Pretty Kreestine."

She started to sigh, then found her breath stolen by the gentle caress of his thumb across her cheek. For a fleeting instant she thought he was going to kiss her again. Instead, he let his hand fall away, and she didn't know what to do with the anticipation he'd left behind.

"Do you have a telephone?" he asked.

"Telephone?" she echoed, staring at him, still aware of the warmth he'd left on her skin.

A grin tugged at his mouth. "Yes, telephone."

She was blushing; she felt the heat and embarrassment stealing over her face. "Telephone," she said, forcing her gaze away. "Of course, it's . . . it's . . ." She glanced around the office, trying to remember where she kept the phone. "It's on the desk. Of course, it's on the desk . . . somewhere on the desk." Her voice trailed off. Lord, what a disaster. She'd never minded it before, but she suddenly hated having her hereditary disorganization exposed to a man whose every movement seemed in tune with the cosmic forces of the universe.

"May I use it?"

"Yes." If she could find it, she silently added, walking over to the desk that she knew resided under the cascades of paper and books. She caught sight of her modem, the phone had to be close. Where had she put the darn thing after she'd talked to Jenny the last time? Sometimes she stashed it in the drawer if she needed more room to work. A couple of times she'd put it on the floor. Only once had she set it in the metal waste-basket. The resulting echo of the ring had convinced her not to use that particular spot again.

He followed her and moved an untidy stack of manuscript she'd been meaning to file away all afternoon, unerringly finding the phone beneath it. He lifted the receiver and began punching in a series of numbers on her wonder of technology. Long distance, she noted. When he finished he set the receiver back into its cradle and looked up at her with an easy grin. "Will you smile, Kreestine?"

The ringing of the phone punctuated her long silence. Without the slightest hesitation or confusion, she realized, he'd set the phone on its speaker mode. Either the far reaches of Nepal were much more technologically advanced than she'd assumed, or her houseguest had spent a fair amount of time in the more modern and cosmopolitan areas of the Far East. Or, he simply was amazingly adept with high-tech gadgets, something she was not. She wished she'd paid more attention to which buttons he'd pushed. Using the speaker feature on her phone was a trick that had eluded her since she'd lost the directions.

"I can't smile on command," she said in response to his strange request.

"Maybe later, then?" His own smile didn't need any incentive, and Kristine found herself responding, her mouth curving up at the corners. "Thank you," he said gravely.

"Sure, anytime." She even laughed a little. She didn't know what to make of him, this elusive stranger who had invaded her life and her home with his forbidden treasures and easy smiles. Except that she was determined to make the most of him. Or rather, the most of his treasures, she hastened to amend. Make the most of him, indeed. The thought was absurd. She, of all women, was the least prepared to make anything out of an overly friendly kiss. Her sexual failings had been neatly categorized once, and once had been enough. More than enough.

"Lois Sheperd's office," a voice came out of the speaker. "May I help you?"

Kristine shot him a surprised glance.

"Lo-eese, please." He grinned at her again, deepening the creases in his lean cheeks.

"May I ask who's calling?"

"Kautilya Carson."

"Hold, please."

"Thank you."

No, Kristine thought, her eyes narrowing in suspicion. He couldn't possibly have called the curator of the largest natural history museum on the West Coast. Given five minutes and a piece of paper, she could have listed twenty museums that would beg for the opportunity to procure what he'd brought out of Tibet. Lois Sheperd of The Natural History Museum of Los Angeles County, Lois Sheperd, curator, would have been the first.

"Kit?" An equally disbelieving feminine voice came on the line.

"*Namaste*, Lo-eese." He picked up one of the many books piled every which way on Kristine's desk and read the spine.

"Kit! You made it!"

"Made it?" He looked at Kristine, one brow cocked in question.

But Lois Sheperd explained before Kristine had the chance. "You arrived without problems."

"No, Lo-eese. I had many problems." He turned to the bookcase and began examining the titles. "But you expected this, no?"

"Well, yes, but if Thomas and I had harbored major doubts, we wouldn't have involved the museums. We knew what you were up against, but we never lost hope."

Who was Thomas? Kristine wondered. And since when was the L.A. museum a part of their project? They hadn't been listed on any of the papers she'd seen, but then neither had Chatren-Ma. The man was more than an outlaw. He was an out-and-out con artist, and he was playing all sides against the middle in some very exalted company. Her professional opinion of him, already heightened by his research, rose another couple of notches. Personally, though, she still didn't know what to make of him.

"You lost the trunks, Lo-eese," he said, and Kristine heard the quiet condemnation in his voice. "This carelessness has created complications." He took one book off the shelf and replaced it with the one in his hand.

"I'm never careless, Kit, never," Lois replied, seemingly unaffected by his censure. "But I will admit to being self-serving at times. We both know why I couldn't' accept the trunks. I'm sure Thomas felt the same. And of course, you found them."

"Naturally."

"Hah! There was nothing natural about the way you—" She paused suddenly. "Where are you?"

"With Kreestine in Colorado." He walked down the length of the bookcase until he found a spot for the second book. Kristine was pleased to discover it wasn't only she he never gave a straight answer to.

On the other hand, Lois didn't sound the least bit pleased. "Kristine? Who is Kristine?"

"A less self-serving woman," he said vaguely. "She is very pretty."

And she'd thought he'd embarrassed her before, Kristine thought, covering her face with one hand.

He'd just told one of the most influential curators in America that she was pretty, not exactly the introduction she'd been imagining all day as she'd gone through his journals and dreamed her little dreams of fame and glory.

"I've never known you to . . ." Lois started to say, then changed her mind. "It doesn't matter, I'm sure. When can you come to Los Angeles?"

He picked another book off the desk and glanced at Kristine. "Do you want to go to Los Angeles?"

Mortified by what Lois Sheperd must be thinking, Kristine mouthed the word "no" then immediately realized her mistake.

"Kreestine says no," he told Lois. "You will come here."

The woman's silent surprise shot through the office, but with no more force than Kristine's. Nobody ordered Lois Sheperd around—except, obviously, Kit Carson.

"So it does matter," Lois said thoughtfully, then reverted to a businesslike tone. "I can be there Monday. Is that too late?"

"No."

"Then I'll see you Monday. What's the address?"

After he'd given Lois the address and had hung up, Kit punched in another series of numbers on the phone, apparently from memory. "May I eat in here, Kreestine?" he asked, looking up at her again. "We have much work to do before Monday and I'd like to get started."

Sure, she thought, why not. Nothing else he did now would surprise her.

She should have known better.

"Thomas Stein's office," a woman said over the speaker. "May I help you?"

Thomas Stein? Kristine thought. *The* Thomas Stein?

"I'm not going to Chicago," she said to Kit to save herself further embarrassment. Then she turned and fled into the kitchen.

Four

Kit confused people besides herself. Kristine saw in the faces of the Thursday morning shoppers. At first glance they dismissed him as a throwback to the sixties, but he always drew second and third glances, and that was where the confusion crept in. He was scrupulously clean, and his demeanor was not one of a lost, searching, or peaceful soul. He was more warrior than saint, though she'd seen in him enough traits of the latter to make her wonder.

The riches encircling his arm revealed wealth in an unaccustomed manner. That wealth was at odds with the roughness of his boots, which Kristine noticed a lot of people bothering to get a look at—especially the women who checked him out from top to bottom.

They had their first disagreement in the produce aisle, shortly after two gawking women ran into each other's carts. One had a toddler strapped into the little seat in front, and Kristine noticed that the little boy loved the bit of action.

"Mama, bang bang? Bang bang, please."

The flustered woman shushed her child and kissed his cheek, her own face flushing a bright pink. "No more bang bang. Excuse me," she said to the other woman, who hadn't quite come back to earth. "Excuse me."

"Oh. Yes. Of course, excuse me."

Their eyes met for an instant, then they simultaneously turned their heads and stared at Kit again. Kristine was beginning to wonder if she had disappeared. Sure, he was intriguing in an exotic sort of way and good looking in any way, but he was just a man. The two women looked back at each other and laughed, a mite breathlessly to Kristine's ears, before going on their way.

She turned to the counter of bananas and started to put a bunch in the cart, then stopped, aghast. Several pounds already layered the bottom of the cart. "Nobody, and I mean nobody, can eat that many bananas."

"I like them," Kit said, and moved over to the melons. He hefted one in each hand, raising them to his nose. Two cantaloupes were within reason, Kristine allowed, but he took four.

She calmly returned three pounds of bananas and two of the melons, and he calmly put them back in the cart.

"I like them."

She had suggested he stay at home while she did the shopping, and if she'd had any idea of how much attention he'd receive or how much trouble he'd be, she would have insisted. Though she doubted it would have done her much good. For some reason he'd been rather insistent himself about accompanying her. She'd muttered something about Tibetan bandits being rare in this particular part of Colorado, but he'd only smiled and followed her out to the car.

They had their second disagreement in the personal hygiene aisle, only because she'd given up at the meat counter. The man was definitely not a vegetarian.

"I think one is enough," she said.

"They are very difficult to find," he said, adding another handful to their burgeoning cart.

"Not in America."

He nodded slowly, as if considering the truth of her statement, then just as slowly laid another handful of toothbrushes in the cart.

"It is a ritual of my first father," he said.

"First father?"

"Before Sang Phala took me away to live with the monks."

Oh, she thought. His first father before the monks. *Right.* She couldn't figure him out for all the gold in China, most of which he seemed to have brought with him. While they'd been working the previous night and that morning, he'd matched her knowledge fact for fact. Yet when it came to plain living on the planet, he was out of his depth. Or more specifically, out of his culture. The practical, and probably rude, thing to do would be to ask a mere hundred or so of the questions tripping over one another in her mind. Practicality had never been her strong suit, though, and rudeness even less so. Besides, prying into his private life implied an intimacy she didn't wish to encourage. They were already living together, for goodness sakes.

In deference to her convoluted logic, she said nothing and added a large supply of toothpaste to their haul. She would simply hand the mystery of Kit Carson over to Jenny to solve. The man's past didn't stand a chance against her assistant's zeal for extra credit. As an added bonus, she'd give points for expediency. The sooner she found out more about him, the better for her peace of mind.

Kit noted the smile forming on Kristine's mouth and the light of curiosity burning like the flame of Muktinath in her eyes. He grinned to himself. It took no special effort on his part to deduce the cause for either. Everything she thought was mirrored on her face. He'd relied on her intelligence, played on her ambitions, and counted on her daring to get him this far. She understood the stakes if not the repercussions of the game she'd fallen into, and he was willing to let her set her own rules—until they clashed with his.

They had their third and final conflict in the checkout lane.

"No," she whispered sharply.

"Help me, please," he said starting to count bracelets. "How many?"

"None. Zero."

The jangling of bracelets as he started to remove them snapped her head around, and she grabbed his arm before she thought. She snatched her hand back, her fingers burning from the heat of his skin. Due to the unreliability of her emotional responses, she had made a firm vow not to instigate any physical encounters.

"This man will not take your bracelets in pay-ment," she said, enunciating every word, "so keep them on your arm, please." The man had money, she knew, all kinds of money, none of which was legal tender in the States. When he'd dumped it out of his chamois bag and into a pile on her kitchen table, she'd spent all of two seconds won-dering how he'd gotten it into the country. Then she'd realized the stupidity of the question. The man had gotten more than yuan, three kinds of rupees, and baht into the country. Lord, she hoped she could pull off her Chatren-Ma coup without getting incriminated by the man's "other talents," as Dean Chambers so delicately put it.

She finished writing out her check and handed it to the clerk.

"He'll take paper before gold?" Kit asked perfectly clearly.

"It's a check, a promise from my bank to pay his," she explained in an undertone designed for subtleness, but his responsive burst of laughter made the attempt fruitless. Heads turned in three lanes, until once more the man with the braid and massive gold bracelets was the absolute center of attention. Kristine smiled weakly at the clerk, wondering if Kit Carson had ever heard the word discretion, let alone figured out how to incorporate it into his life.

Okay, Kristine thought several hours later, so far so good. He had his neat, collated piles over there, and she had her not-so-neat piles over here—and suppertime was only a heartbeat away. Thank heaven.

How a man could be relaxed enough to wear a braid down to his whatever and more gold than King Tut, and still be such a stickler for organization was beyond her. He looked so loose and free, from his quick, easy smiles down to the hoops on his boots. But those smiles, she'd discovered, had more edges than curves, and she was sure he was in imminent danger of wearing out his patient edge.

"I need to cross-reference the February and March daily journals into the Lamaist Shrine catalogue," he said. He walked over to her side of the office and dropped down on his haunches next to where she'd set up shop on the floor.

"Check, and check." She dug the two bound volumes out of her untidy stacks and handed them to him, breathing a silent sigh of relief. More than once she'd had to scramble to find his requests.

"Thank you, Kreestine." His most patient smile played at the corners of his mouth, mesmerizing her. "Do you also have the shrine catalogue?"

"Yes, it's right . . ." She tore her gaze away from him and searched the piles of folios and folders. He was too close, his shoulder almost brushing hers, his thigh definitely touching her arm. How was she supposed to concentrate when he was practically breathing on her? "I had finished filling in the April data and was going onto May, but I couldn't find May, so I set the catalogue aside."

He shifted his body an inch closer, leaning across her to pick up the catalogue. "Thank you, Kreestine, and do not concern yourself with May. There are no daily journals for May."

He slowly rose to his feet and moved back to his

side of the office, becoming instantly engrossed in the catalogue and leaving her to wonder what it was about him that so fascinated her.

She knew a lot of men, all kinds of men. She worked with them, taught them, and on occasion flunked them without batting an eyelash. But she'd never met or seen one like Kit Carson. The mystery of him went beyond his past. It was more than skin-deep. It was more than his kiss, though that alone made him unique in her experience. No one had ever turned her into jelly with just a kiss, or anything else for that matter.

With a little hummph, she turned her attention back to her work, spending a few minutes tidying up her area and sipping her cold coffee. She decided to warm it up and walked over to the pot she kept in the office. While she was there she sharpened her pencils, opened an envelope from the morning's mail, and filed the bill in the URGENT bin on her multilayered desk baskets.

Now what had she been doing before he'd interrupted her? she wondered. May, that was right. She'd been looking for the May journals—which he'd told her didn't exist.

"Why not?" she murmured aloud. It was more a question to herself than to him, but he answered.

"It didn't seem wise to make a record of where I was and what I was doing in May. But you need not worry. I have the information I promised you, and the lack of a journal will not affect the published account of the historical sites."

"Oh," was all she managed to reply. The man had the memory of an elephant. Or he was telepathic, a possibility that was seeming less ridiculous all the time.

He'd been at Chatren-Ma in May, of course, and under circumstances she wouldn't want written down either, for fear the journals would fall into the wrong hands or even the right hands. Still, she felt cheated out of the best part of the story. She'd come across vague references to the monastery in her professional studies, and more than one account of hearsay in another scholar's work, along the lines of "an old man told of a man he knew whose brother-in-law, etcetera, etcetera." Pure fiction for all practical purposes, but to have had a firsthand account, and from someone with Kit's capacity for remembering even trivial details, would have been incredible.

But then, that was what he'd promised her, a firsthand account, to do with as she wished, all for the price of three meals a day and a bed. Not only that, he'd insisted on reimbursing her for the meals as soon as his finances took a turn to the legally exchangable side. She'd made worse bargains in her life.

After dinner Kit startled her again, but in a thoroughly different manner. The sun had barely set when he rose quickly from his chair, crossed the office to the door that led to the deck, and slipped outside. If she hadn't seen him, she certainly wouldn't have heard him. Not even the silver rings on his boots had made a sound, or maybe she'd grown accustomed to the light jangling. No other explanation made sense.

Neither did the way he disappeared on the other side of the glass door. She held her curiosity in check for about thirty seconds, then followed him. The night was dark, waiting for the moon to rise, but light from the door and the living room windows cast a soft glow over the wood deck.

She padded around the perimeter, skinned her knee on the picnic table bench, cursed softly, and continued around to the sunroom side of the house.

"You felt it too?" she heard Kit say.

Stopping at the sound of his voice, she was on the verge of answering—if only to figure out where he was—when she realized he wasn't talking to her.

Mancos loped over to the stand of aspen trees skirting the driveway, the low growl in his throat turning to a whine.

Felt what? she wondered. She hadn't felt anything except the scrape on her knee and a bit of unease over his disappearing act.

"We must be careful, eh?" His voice drifted up to where she stood on the deck, and her uneasiness increased.

The man was no fool. He'd been proving that to her all day long, and if he was going to be careful, maybe she should be too. But careful of what? The wind?

"The Turk is fast," he said as if in answer, "especially when he rides alone. If he comes we must be faster, Mancos." The words were delivered like a lesson, patient but serious, heavy with an importance Kristine found difficult to match in herself.

If he'd spoken about international antiquities thieves, or some man in a suit and tie trading contraband, she might have been able to rustle up some extra wariness. But he spoke of bandits, and a third world bandit at that. Everything she'd read about such men, from *National Geographic* to professional journals, depicted them as local people, usually poor and uneducated, who dealt only with the next man up on the scale.

She admitted she might be misunderstanding Kit, or that someone called "the Turk" might possibly be the next man up on the scale, but she figured if Kit Carson was going to be jumping at the wind, their project would be better served by someone else keeping both feet firmly on the ground. Not really her forte, she also admitted, but no one could say Kristine Richards didn't come through in a pinch.

She slipped back inside before he caught her out on the deck, listening to him talk to her dog. She talked to Mancos, too, but their conversations tended to revolve around food or the lack thereof. She'd never considered the animal a confidant, and he drooled too much to make a good cuddle-buddy. Kit Carson, on the other hand, would make a very good cuddly-buddy.

Oh, grow up, Kristine, she told herself, irritated with the one-track expressway he'd made of her mind with just one kiss.

Kit waited until she was gone before he delivered his final warning to the dog. He'd known she had followed him, and would have been disappointed if she hadn't. It would have meant he'd misjudged her, and misjudgments of any kind were exactly what wasn't allowed for the next few days.

He didn't want her frightened or losing sleep. He

wanted her as fresh and excited as she'd been all day. She was the most intriguing mixture of confidence and doubts. He'd panicked her a couple times, asking for files she'd misplaced, but he had soon realized she misplaced everything. He also made her nervous when he got close to her. He felt her awareness heighten, all her senses come into play, but it was a good nervous. Not good enough, not yet, but soon.

Growing up with a scarcity of possessions and the unbending discipline of the monastery, he found her Bohemian ways a rare challenge to keep up with and strangely fascinating. He kept wondering when and if she was actually going to lose one of the journals he'd risked his life to compile.

He liked watching her, watching her work, watching her think, watching her tuck ever-straying tendrils of hair behind her ear. More than once he'd been tempted to reach out and perform the task himself, not because the loose strands bothered him, but solely for the opportunity to touch her.

He wanted to touch her. In truth, he'd thought of little else since he'd kissed her. The pale creaminess of her skin was like a magnet to his fingers, the soft lushness of her lips like a lodestone to his mouth. Her dark mane of hair seemed to cry out for his hands to smooth it across his pillow, or wrap it around his fist as he drew her to him.

He knew some called him a barbarian, but none had made him feel more so than the woman with the violet eyes. He'd always considered himself the most civilized of men, more civilized than those who chose to call him barbarian and outlaw. This was the legacy of years of contemplation, of hours and often days of meditation on many things not easily apparent.

But, tonight . . . tonight he wished he could take her for his own. She appeared untouched, though he knew the mores of Western culture made that supposition doubtful. He also knew he wouldn't have her tonight. His instincts were very sure of that.

He turned his attention back to the dog, scratching him behind the ears. "Stay close to her, Mancos. Guard her well, and if the need arises, call for me. Can you do that?"

The dog answered with a series of rumbling howls, bringing a grin to Kit's face.

"Good dog."

Inside the house, Kristine scrambled to her feet. What were they doing out there? Trying to wake half the mountain?

In her haste, she knocked over her coffee cup and barely saved one of his manuscripts from a soaking. She threw half a dozen tissues on the floor and turned back to the door, when the phone rang.

She hesitated for a moment before curiosity won out.

"Hello?" she said into the receiver.

"Kris, it's John." The voice sounded through the whole room, and she eyed the phone, wondering which button to push to get it off of the speaker.

Rudeness, not ignorance, compelled her to ask, "John who?" when she knew darn well John who.

"Garraty."

She had all kinds of buttons to choose from,

direct-dial buttons, hold buttons, on-off buttons, a battery-dead button that wasn't really a button at all, and a couple of other miscellaneous buttons and switches. She pushed one and the line went dead. It was a solution of sorts, but not for long.

The phone rang again.

"Hello?"

"Okay, okay. You've made your point."

"I'm not trying to make a point, Dr. Garraty. I'm trying to—" She pushed another button and was blessed with silence.

The phone rang once more. She knew it was him. It had to be. But maybe it was someone else, like her mother. It might even be her sister. She hadn't talked to Sarah all week.

"Hello?"

"Dammit, Kris. If you hang up on me again, I'll just come up there."

It was him.

"I didn't hang up on you," she said. "I've got a problem with the speaker phone." A problem she didn't dare have again, not with the possibility of him driving up there hanging over her head.

"Well, quite fooling with it and I'll bet you don't have any more problems."

He was so smart, she thought sourly. Smart enough to dump her, smart enough to cause a scandal that had almost torn her family apart. He'd not only dumped her, he'd dumped her for her own cousin, and worse yet, he'd gotten said cousin pregnant while he'd still been engaged to Kristine. There had been so much finger counting that year, her relatives had almost worn themselves out. She had to put up with him and his brood at Christmas and the Fourth of July. She certainly didn't like having to put up with him in her own home, not even on long distance.

"What do you want?" she asked. It came out as "waddyawant," with hardly a break and not even a whisper of politeness.

"I'm calling to see how you're doing."

He was so thoughtful, she mused, glaring at the phone. Thoughtful enough to mortify her right out of her assistant professorship at the University of Colorado. She'd stupidly resigned in a fit of outraged pride and had been fighting ever since to make up the lost ground.

"I'm fine," she said. "How's Lisa?" Low blow, Kristine, she told herself. Really tacky. She swore she wouldn't do it again.

"Everybody's fine. Lisa and the kids are looking forward to the picnic on the Fourth. She's got a new potato salad everybody's going to go crazy over."

"No doubt," Kristine said without even half the possible sarcasm. He was so proud of Lisa's salads. He could have had brilliance, but he'd settled for potato salad—and great sex, if two kids in four years and another on the way was any indication.

"But I didn't call to talk about potato salad," he said.

"Thank you." A touch of sarcasm slipped in.

"I called to talk about Carson."

Playing dumb didn't come easily to her, but she stretched herself. "Carson who?"

"Kit Carson. I know he's here in Colorado, and I don't think you should get involved."

Well, well, she thought, imagine that. John Garraty a day late and a dollar short. Make that two days late.

"The smartest thing you could do right now is dump the project," he continued. "I'd be willing to talk to Dean Chambers and have the contract shifted over to Boulder. We're better prepared to handle the heat. And Carson is hot, Kris, don't fool yourself. They don't call him an outlaw for nothing."

"Hmmm," she murmured, not having a glib remark handy. John didn't know how close to the truth he was.

"The guy has been walking the line between research and treasure hunting for so long, he probably has grooves in the soles of his boots. Who knows what he's really up to? Who knows what he found out there?"

"Careful, Dr. Garraty. Your aspirations are starting to leak through your concern."

"The Chinese are mad for a reason."

"I've heard the rumors," she admitted, dropping into her swivel chair.

"Everybody has heard the rumors." John's voice grew harder, less conciliatory. "I'm more interested in the facts."

"Which facts are these, Kreestine?"

She jumped out of her chair. How long had Kit been standing in the doorway?

"Who's that?" John asked, sounding confused.

How much had he heard? she wondered, staring at him.

"Kris?"

"What?" She continued looking at Kit, not knowing how much to explain of what he may or may not have heard.

"Is there someone else there?" John asked.

Etiquette was the only answer to the situation.

Kristine took a deep breath and said, "John, I'd like you to meet Kit Carson."

With predictable arrogance, John didn't sound the least bit embarrassed. Quite the contrary. He started right in with the hard sell. "John Garraty, Kit, Middle East specialist for the University of Colorado. We've been hearing a lot about you lately."

"So it seems," Kit replied, not at all sure he liked what he'd overheard. He didn't mind the references to himself; he'd certainly heard worse. But the edge in Kristine's voice told him there was something between the Middle East specialist and her that went beyond a professional relationship. He hadn't considered such a possibility.

"You know," John went on, orally filling in his resume, "I've traveled quite extensively in your part of the world, the East. I directed an expedition to Petra and I've worked with a couple of people out of Karachi, Dr. Singh and Dr. Alexander." He dropped the two famous names with ease, but with no noticeable effect.

"No, I didn't know this," Kit said, watching a blush spread across Kristine's cheeks.

John ignored the literal interpretation and continued. "As a matter of fact, Kristine and I had planned a trip to Nepal. We were hoping to get into Tibet, but you know how tricky that can be."

"This I do know." Kristine saw his eyes narrow at her from across the room as he asked her, "When did you plan this trip, *bahini*?"

She didn't understand the word, but it sounded disturbingly like an endearment when spoken in his deep, singsong voice, and it did little to restore the composure John had ripped out from under her. The Nepal trip was supposed to have been their honeymoon—he and Lisa had gone to Hawaii, showing little or no imagination—and she couldn't believe he'd had the nerve to mention it.

Kit felt the underlying tension in the room rise again, and suddenly he knew one more thing about her: John Garraty had hurt her. His own reaction to that knowledge caught him off-guard, causing him to stumble inside on some hidden plane.

He knew how to cope with anger. He'd learned in the monastery to dismiss it as a wrong path, and learned in the outside world to use it only for his own survival. But jealousy was a perplexing unknown, and a day, or even an hour, earlier he would have thought himself incapable of such a worthless emotion. He didn't take the revelation lightly.

"It was a long time ago," Kristine said, filling in the endless silence and wondering what it was she saw darkening Kit's eyes.

"Apparently not long enough, *bahini*," he said, his voice an unusual monotone of strain. With a slight touching of his palms and a light jangle of bracelets, he bowed, then strode out of the office.

"All of us over here in Boulder are interested in your latest project," John said, oblivious to the absence of his chosen audience, "and we're able to offer you—"

"He's gone, John," Kristine interrupted.

"Gone where?"

"To bed, probably," she said without thinking, but the meaning wasn't lost on John.

"Dammit, Kris. What are you up—"

She pushed one button, then another, and another, then unplugged the phone from the wall.

Slumping down in her chair, she finished the last inch of coffee in her cup as she stared at the door. She'd been warned three times, by Dean Chambers, by Jenny, and now by John.

But she wasn't going to back off. Wild horses and rabid dogs couldn't make her.

Five

Kristine, stabbed again at the roasted chicken sitting on a platter in the middle of her kitchen table. She shouldn't have bothered. Kit hadn't shown up for breakfast, he hadn't shown up for lunch, and it didn't look like he was going to show up for dinner. The chicken was cold, the peas had dried up, and the biscuits were turning to rocks. She really shouldn't have bothered. Lord only knew why she had. She'd never impressed anyone with her culinary skills.

What was he doing up there in his room? Starting a religious fast? She looked out the window at her detached garage. An evening breeze fanned the pine trees, sending waves of golden pollen dancing through the sunset like handfuls of glitter.

Figuring she might as well give in sooner rather than later, she pushed away from the table and let herself out the back door. The man had to eat, and they had work to do.

Her palms were sweating as she climbed the outside stairs to the second-floor apartment. Her pulse quickened as she faced the door. She lifted her hand to knock, then hesitated.

Maybe she imagined hearing the word "enter", but after a moment she slipped out of the fading light and into the warm dark room.

Her eyes adjusted slowly; her heart didn't adjust at all. He sat opposite the door on a softly worn sheepskin, naked except for a pair of black shorts. Perspiration glistened on his forehead and closed eyelids. Dampness graced the curved muscle's in his arms, the breadth of his chest, and the long length of his legs. The soles of his bare feet rested upturned on his inner thighs.

The quiet, peaceful beauty of him took her breath away, and it was long seconds before she remembered to exhale. She shouldn't have come, but neither could she force herself to leave.

The breeze blew in through an open window and lightly tousled the loose, shorter hair framing his face. The strands spread like a feather across his cheekbone, drawing her gaze back to his face. His eyes were now open, but no less blind than they had been before.

She automatically took a step back, then stopped, held in place by her own overreacting instincts. He didn't want her to leave. Or did he? She wasn't sure . . . of anything.

She shifted her gaze away, lightening the spell but not breaking it. Wiping her palms on the front of her jeans, she looked around his room, for he'd definitely made it his own. The trunks and bed filled most of the floor space, and a hundred other objects covered them. Brass bells, a Tibetan prayer wheel, rugs and tapestries, a copper bowl, a pottery dish filled with turquoise nuggets, another of tourmaline. An eerily familiar gold mask, a chunk of rock crystal bigger than both of her fists. The treasure trove of an adventurer with eclectic tastes.

Scattered among the antiquities were signs of modern man: his razor and toothbrushes, a backpack-size butane stove, a sack of tea, and a typewriter.

She glanced at him, found his eyes closed again, and took the steps necessary to bring her to one of the trunks. The piece of paper in the typewriter was blank. She made a soft sound of relief; she didn't really want to be a snoop. She took another light step, then another, easing deeper into the private sanctuary he'd made of her extra room. She sifted her fingers through the semi-precious stones. She touched his prayer wheel, then kept herself from doing the same to the worn jeans and black tunic thrown over one of the trunks. Her hand trailed over the gold mask, and the sense of familiarity returned stronger than before. The gilded bridge of a straight nose, the warm metallic of sculpted cheekbones and the curve of a mouth she knew better than she should. Her fingers paused and her lips parted softly on a gasp of recognition . . . *Kautilya*. His name echoed in her mind and found an answer in the air.

Kreestine.

She whirled around, her heart pounding, the mask clasped in her hands. She tried to run, but it was too late for running. Her feet froze to the floor, numbed by the weight of his ancient gaze. She'd been wrong to come, and given another chance, she would have let him go hungry for the night.

Kit wasn't in the mood for second chances. Hours of meditation had done little to lessen his anger or increase his understanding of the other feelings she'd given him. A month from home hadn't changed him as much as two days in her company. He wanted her, had planned from their first kiss to have her, but he hadn't expected to lose himself in the bargain. He hadn't expected changes wrought by desire. He'd never felt changes before.

What was it about her? She was beautiful, yes, but many women were beautiful, and she seemed unaware of the fact. She'd done none of the subtle flirting he'd encountered with other women who wanted him. Yet he'd felt the sensual curiosity in her hidden glances. Her clothes were plain, unsuitable in color and style to enhance her appeal. A deliberate choice on her part, he was sure, and that had only increased his fascination—until he'd listened to John Garraty and determined the cause.

She had a quick, bright mind, so unlike the steady deepness of the monks and Sang Phala, so much broader than the other women he'd met, except for Lois. But his relationship with Lois was business and hard, without the softness he'd felt from the first moment with Kristine. Her vulnerabilities, which she tried so valiantly to conceal, attracted him as much as her strengths. Maybe more so.

He'd discovered all of this in his time alone and still had no peace.

Why have you come to me?

Kristine heard the question clearly, more clearly than if he'd spoken aloud, and in a sudden flash of enlightenment she understood the true depth of his power, of his energy. She stumbled backward, coming up against the trunk. She'd read volumes of theory and hearsay, from Polo to Maraini, about the metaphysical mysteries of Tibetan Lamaism, and if he levitated she was going to run like hell, whether her feet refused to move or not.

"Impossible for one with my limited knowledge and commitment, Kreestine," he assured her in his deep, soft voice. "You have no reason to fear."

"D-don't do that," she stammered, giving them both enough credit to know something had happened, something very unusual.

"I can do nothing you do not allow. You are very . . . open." He spoke the last word in an intimate, husky whisper, loading it with meaning beyond the obvious. "You called my name, and I answered, nothing more."

She believed him. She always believed him, but her pulse didn't slow down. In fact, when he rose from the floor with his particularly fluid grace and walked toward her, it picked up a good bit.

"Why have you come to me?" he asked again, moving ever closer, narrowing the space between them. He filled her vision with his smoothly muscled chest and arms. Gold bracelets glinted, picking up the last stray beams of sunlight, contrasting with the dark satin of his skin and the soft pelt of hair tracing a path to his shorts.

"Your dinner was getting cold," she said, giving in to an undeniable need for rock-solid reality. Her mind, though, was still racing around the startling realization of his invasion into her thoughts. Just how many years had he spent in that monastery? she wondered.

"Too many." He took another silent step, his gaze never leaving hers. "Why have you come to me?"

"Stop it!" she exclaimed more angry than afraid. She had enough problems keeping everything in her mind straight without him adding to the chaos. But he kept gliding closer, and the question in his eyes demanded an answer. "We need to work," she said. "We've already lost most of the day." Her voice grew ever softer, her words ever slower, and she felt the padlock of his trunk press against the back of her thigh.

"No more then, as you wish." He touched her face with both hands and brushed her hair behind her ears. She hadn't twisted the black mane into a tight knot. A pleased, yet half sly smile curved his mouth, and her heart sank along with her last ounce of anger, chased by the darkness of his eyes into oblivion.

The muscles in his arms flexed as he cupped her face in his palms. He was going to kiss her, and she hadn't come for his kiss. Or had she?

The question proved moot. She didn't run when he grazed her cheek with his mouth. Instead, her eyes drifted closed and her knees weakened. She didn't run when his caress roamed down the side of her nose to her mouth. Her lips parted, waiting for his kiss, and she wondered at the magic of his touch.

His heat enveloped her in a cocoon of masculine scents, tantalizing her with a promise he didn't fulfill. His mouth hovered above hers, and he touched her only with the softness of his breath and the palpable desire she sensed flowing off him and into her.

The wait was maddening. Her body pleaded with her to move, to close the spare inch separating them. She licked her lips and felt the barest touch of his mouth on the tip of her tongue, the almost imperceptible tightening of his hands on her face. He was that close, holding her but not taking her, and she was unravelling inside, her breath coming harder and faster.

Her hands wrapped tighter around the mask, and all the while she knew it was him she longed to hold; to feel the breadth of his shoulders beneath her palms, to tangle her fingers in the soft luxury of his hair and feel the cord of auburn silk sliding down the back of his neck. He wasn't an outlaw, he was an enchanter. No pious monk, but a shaman skilled in the arts of seduction. Without even a kiss he had her aroused, panting, melting inside.

His hands tunneled into her hair, drawing her closer until his mouth touched hers, and his words whispered against her lips. "Will you sleep in my bed tonight, Kreestine?"

With her eyes closed she couldn't see his smile, but she felt it in all its barbaric arrogance. He was playing with her. He had no intention of kissing her. He only wanted to see how far she'd go.

Even after discerning the nature of his game, she found herself hard-pressed to move away. If she gave into her every raging impulse and kissed him, he'd have his answer, and she knew she couldn't carry through to the end. He was so close, so mesmerizingly close. All she wanted was a kiss, one kiss like the one he'd given her on the deck, a kiss she couldn't pay for in the currency he requested. Was one kiss too much to ask for?

"Not to much, *bahini,* too little," he murmured, his mouth teasing hers.

Her eyes opened slowly and she angled her head back. "You said . . . you said you wouldn't."

"I didn't."

"Then how?"

His lips brushed hers lightly, barely, not nearly enough. "My heart is open, too, Kreestine, and it hears yours on every beat."

Now was the time to run, she thought, before she fell completely under his sensual spell and made a total fool out of herself. No one did it better than she in these situations. She found strength in her memories of awkwardness and John's neatly summed-up farewell speech. Kit's kiss for her love-making? Not even a third world barbarian would find much pleasure in such a poor bargain.

Moving sideways, she slipped free of his hands. Easily, because he let her go, and with difficulty, because the backs of her fingers brushed against his taut abdomen. She lingered there for a fraction of a second, feeling the soft hair that swirled in a glorious path around his navel before plunging beneath the running shorts.

Kit let her go, but not easily. The longing and denial he sensed in her made emotional mud of her thoughts, and without his touch, her willing-ness, or the grace of his meditative state, he found it impossible to see further. He rarely wished he'd stayed longer under the tutelage of Sang Phala, but then he'd never felt jealousy before.

She paced across the room, halting in front of his bed. For a moment he was tempted to nudge her forward, to walk up behind her and caress the womanly curves of her hips and urge her, with his thoughts and his hands, onto his bed. But such a breach of faith was beyond his conscience. The arts of persuasion were not for such as this.

He reached for his jeans instead and tugged

them on, ignoring their unaccustomed tightness. This too shall pass, he thought, grinning wryly at himself. But it was a pained smile at best.

The sound of his zipper, hushed and grating, sent a shiver down Kristine's spine and a flood of warmth through her body. She unconsciously raised the gold mask and fanned herself, forcing her gaze to remain locked on his bed. Another bad choice, she immediately realized. She'd given him sheets, a couple of quilts, and some pillows, but it was his additions that bewitched her with forbidden fantasies.

An uneven spread of sewn-together sheepskins, the wool lush and buttery looking, lay across the bottom of the bed, primitive and sensual. She knew it would smell of him. Without any effort on her part she imagined him lying there, his dark skin contrasting with the pale wool, his muscles flexing as he arranged himself for comfort and love, his braid falling over his shoulder as he reached for one of his elaborately stitched tapestry pillows and laid it beneath her head, his mouth lowering to hers as he covered her body with his.

The fanning mask picked up in speed, and still she felt herself melting in places John had once told her were drier than the Sahara in summer. He spoke from experience, having been to North Africa in July, and she'd believed him all these years—until she looked at Kit Carson's bed.

She heard him slip into his black tunic, and she swore she could hear every single button slide through his calloused fingers. She was on emotional overload, super sensitized, and he hadn't even kissed her.

The jangling of his bracelets increased, and she

knew he was rolling his sleeves, exposing those vein-tracked forearms. How had she gotten herself into such a mess? And how did she get back out? Just say good-bye and dart out the door?

No, that wouldn't do. She needed to rectify the situation, get them back on a professional level. She turned, but any intelligent thought she might have pulled together faded away. He was wrapping his heavy leather belt around his hips, and her gaze was captured by the intimate movements of his hands.

Kit stopped in the act of buckling, surprised and strangely hurt by the stark yearning on her face. He felt the pain and confusion of her wanting, and his anger at Dr. John Garraty, Middle East specialist, increased. He contemplated dropping his belt to the floor and taking her for his own in a manner that would replace the pain with pleasure and completely wipe out any confusion she harbored about the making of love.

Or he could give her time. Few decisions in his life had been as difficult, and Sang Phala had taught him nothing about the taking of women. He'd learned it all on his own. His knowledge had stood him well over the years, but Kristine was quite different from the other women he'd known. Concubine . . . He couldn't have been further off the mark.

The acceptance of his first mistake enabled him to back away emotionally. He finished slipping the belt through its loop. "I'm sorry I ruined our dinner. Let me take you out."

She nodded. She'd do anything to get out of there.

"Good. We'll start our work again in the morning. We still have two good days."

Two days, then what? she wondered, stumbling ahead of him out the door. She didn't need him to write up the historical research. She was in the process of duplicating his journals, and he had triple copies of his photographs and the negatives. Any conferencing they needed to do could be accomplished by phone, with her alone in her mountain house and him—where? Where in the whole wide world would he go when he left her?

She had only herself to blame, Kristine thought. She stood in the darkened doorway of the bar and wished she'd chosen more wisely. The neon promise of hamburgers and beer had lured Kit in there, and she'd followed, foolishly. A redneck bar on the backside of the reservoir, full of drugstore cowboys and a few of the real thing, wasn't the best place to bring a man with a braid and bracelets. The blatant, aggressive stares following them around the room proved her point.

Every farm-equipment manufacturer and feed supplier in the States was well represented on baseball caps pulled low over a dozen foreheads. The Stetsons and Baileys were pulled even lower, especially the black ones. She felt distinctly uncomfortable, though she'd been in the bar before. She'd come with a couple of girlfriends one night, and had been handily welcomed and two-stepped around the dance floor. She and Grant had stopped off after their last date and been ignored. But Kit created animosity with his exotic looks and foreign attire. If she could feel it, his instincts must be racing.

"Interesting place," he said, his voice the epitome of calm as he pulled out her chair.

She sat down and grabbed a menu. "The hamburgers are good. The Mexican food will probably kill you." Didn't he know he was the focal point of all those beady-eyed glares?

He laughed. "Then we'll have hamburgers. We're too young to die tonight, Kreestine."

Apparently not, she thought, burying her face in the menu.

The waitress took her sweet time about coming for their order of hamburgers and beer, but once she showed up, she seemed disinclined to leave. Kristine didn't have any trouble figuring out why.

"You're not from around here, are you, sugar?" she asked Kit.

"No. I come from Nepal," "Sugar" told her, smiling one of his friendlier smiles. He had a thousand of them, and Kristine figured he'd used a good half-dozen on the nymphet blond already. She was poured into a black and lime-green Lycra top that was more appropriate for the gym than a public restaurant. At least most of her was poured into it. A fair portion of cleavage just wouldn't fit. Slim-hipped in a pair of painted-on jeans and busty— some women had all the luck, Kristine thought, feeling gauche in her mustard-yellow blouse. The blouse hadn't been cheap, but it felt like a big rag when she compared it to the sexy lines of Lycra.

"I had a boyfriend once, a climber," the waitress said. "He went to Nepal. Didn't come back, though." The girl rested one booted foot on top of the other and leaned against the table, effectively blocking

Kristine from the conversation and blowing any chance she had of a good tip. That was a small consolation to Kristine. Very small.

"Many men do not return from the mountains," Kit said. "I'm sorry."

"Oh, he didn't die, sugar. He just didn't come back. But hey, as long as Nepal keeps sending us men like you, what's to miss?"

"There are no others in Nepal like me."

A low, throaty chuckle preceded the waitress's reply as she used one of those slim hips to push off the table. "Honey, there aren't many like you anywhere."

To his everlasting credit, Kit didn't follow the cute sway of the girls bottom down the length of the barroom, but when he spoke, Kristine almost wished he had.

"Who is John Garraty?"

"John Garraty? she repeated, her voice leaden.

"Did I mispronounce the name?" he asked with a lift of his eye brows.

"No," she busied herself with a random search of her purse, looking for an excuse. For the first time she understood why so many women carried compacts and lipstick. They were handy things to hide behind.

"Who is he?"

"A professor at the university in Boulder, just like he said."

Their beers arrived, giving her a moment of reprieve, but only a moment. After a couple of sugar this's and sugar that's, the waitress sashayed back to the bar.

"He's a friend of yours?"

"Not exactly." She bet the waitress had two

compacts and three lipsticks in her purse. Kristine had to make do with an old tube of Chapstick.

"Then why did you plan a long journey with him?"

She glanced up. "It was a mistake."

"Good." A very satisfied smile followed his pronouncement, and he lifted his beer to his mouth.

Kristine dropped the lip balm back in her purse, unused, and sighed. She'd been crazy to tangle herself up with him, *Kāh-gyur*, Chatren-Ma, kisses, non-kisses, and all. One more "sugar" and she'd probably belt that waitress. She'd lost her appetite, and she couldn't wait to get home and burn her blouse. He'd done nothing but add upheaval to a life she usually managed to keep in a state of constant disorientation all by herself.

And to top it all off, he *could* read her mind. If things were going to get any worse, she didn't want to be around when they did.

Six

The hamburgers arrived hot, greasy, and dripping with cheese, just the way she liked them. Too bad she couldn't eat, Kristine thought. She pushed her french fries around the plate, working herself up for a question.

"What did you mean when you said you were taken away?" There, she'd said it. She looked up, waiting for Kit's answer. When he didn't immediately reply, she gave him another hint. "By Sang Phala? Your second father?"

Kit had met a few people with blue eyes, not many, but enough to know that hers were rare not only in their violet shade, but in their inherent warmth. They pulled at him on that same hidden plane his jealousy had discovered, asking for a truth he seldom gave.

But this woman no sooner asked than he discovered a need to answer.

"Sang Phala came for me when I was nine," he

said, holding her gaze. "He paid the Khampas—the warrior bandits—dearly, trading the life of his brother's son for mine." He softened the harsh reality of his words with a slight smile as he picked up his beer. "He regretted the trade many times when I was a boy. I did not make a proper novice."

Watching her lean forward, her hands clasped tightly in her lap, trying to hide her shock, he broadened his grin. She'd be horrified if she knew what a poor job she was doing.

"Trading his nephew? Why?" Her voice had the purely feminine mixture of breathlessness and small catches he found so sweet . . . and erotic. He'd spent the night dreaming of her voice whispering close to him in the dark, breathless with pleasure and catching each time he moved inside her. He shifted restlessly in his chair, once again surprised at the powerful ease of his response to her.

"An old promise to the old man my father became after my mother died giving birth to me," he explained, forcing his concentration back to the conversation and the facts he'd long ago accepted. "In the few years we spent together, until I was seven, I don't think he ever forgave me for being the cause of his loss. Sang Phala was much more generous in that respect, but in no others. He eventually beat the wildness out of me, and in the end I did learn."

"And then you ran away?"

"And then I ran away," he agreed before taking another long swallow of beer.

"What happened to your first father?"

"He was killed by a rifle on Thorong La." He shrugged, a slight lifting of one shoulder. "There were many such misunderstandings on the high passes after the Chinese invasion."

"You call murder a misunderstanding?" Her voice rose to an incredulous degree.

"It is a sin, but one others will pay for." He knew the words sounded callous, but he'd spoken the simple truth.

"Who? Who will pay?"

"I will never know. He wasn't killed in our camp. The Khampas denied any responsibility, though they were the ones who came for me. Sang Phala found me two years later." To ease her distress, he tried to explain further. "My father chose his life. He chose to take my mother with him into a wild land. He chose the place of my birth. He chose to sacrifice himself in the name of scholarly research. I did not choose these things for him, Kreestine. I cannot live with regrets for his mistakes."

Scholarly research in Tibet, Kristine mused. An American murdered in Nepal . . . She put the information together in her mind, then added a guess at his age. Slowly, she sank back in her chair. All of the pieces fit, and she felt like an idiot for not having put them together earlier.

"Dwayne Carson was your father," she said.

Kit lifted one eyebrow. "He never published his work, and his research was lost. How do you know his name?"

"Bertolli mentioned him in *A Land of Snows*, credited him with finding the tomb of Nachukha." Suddenly the mystery of Kit Carson no longer existed. She felt relieved, a little disappointed, and inexplicably sad. She'd discerned no emotional scars in him, but at one time he must have hurt badly, as a child, when the wounds of life cut much more deeply.

Kit reached across the table and took her hands into both of his. "Sang Phala healed me well, Kreestine. There is no need for sadness. And as for the other . . ." A slow smile lifted one corner of his mouth. "There is much still to discover."

"Don't . . . don't do that, please." She pulled her hands free, disturbed by the clarity of his understanding. She'd have to watch herself very carefully around him, and she'd never been any good at watching herself. More often than not, words hit her mouth at the same time they hit her brain. In either case, she wasn't safe from him.

Kit reached for her again, for no other reason than that he wanted to touch her, to feel the vibrancy of her life and the satin smoothness of her skin. Her thick lashes hid her eyes from him, but even so he felt her compassion for a stranger who wished to become more. Soft of heart and strong of mind, with a passion tamped so far down inside her, he doubted she knew it was there, she drew him ever stronger, ever closer, "I think the lady said no, mister." A meaty hand landed palm down on the table, jiggling the beer bottles. "Or is it miss?"

Kit and Kristine both looked up at the intruder, but only one gaze was wide-eyed with surprise. Kit remained calm as he assessed the size—quite large—and the sensibilities—quite crude—of the man he'd felt approaching their table. He wore a rumpled flannel shirt, the sleeves rolled up over hairy forearms, and a pair of dirty jeans hanging low beneath a broad belly. A mop of unruly brown hair stuck out from beneath his baseball cap.

"You have misunderstood," Kit said. "Leave us, please." He returned his attention to Kristine.

"You haven't answered my question, *miss*." The insult was delivered in a slurred baritone drawl, and the man planted another hand on the table, leaning closer. He reached up and flicked Kit's braid. "Where'd you get your pigtail, son? Or should I be calling you girly-girl?"

"You may call me Kautilya," Kit said, his voice losing a trace of his lilt, "and I wear the plait by choice."

"Well, it's mighty pretty, girly-girl. How about if'n I take it as a kind of souvenir? I could hang it on the wall with my hunting trophies." The big man laughed, inordinately amused by his own joke.

"You would not be the first to try," Kit said softly.

Kristine instantly recalled his chamois bag and the long cord of auburn hair woven into the silk and leather strap. Someone had more than tried, she thought. They'd succeeded.

"Yep," the intruder said. "The more I think about it, the more I like the idea, girly-girl." The man's voice lowered to match Kit's, and he pulled a pocket knife out of his jeans. His hand was unsteady. Kristine didn't know what frightened her more, the little knife, or the wavering hand holding it. "Now you just sit real still like and I'll be real careful not to cut you."

The man was drunk, his gray eyes bloodshot, and he must be crazy to boot, she thought. Kit didn't have the look of a man easily intimidated. Quite the contrary. Belligerent glances were one thing, but any fool would have kept his distance. She should've known better than to bring him in there. The culture shock was obviously too much for these life forms on the low end of the food chain.

"Let's go," she said, digging in her purse and throwing a twenty-dollar bill on the table. The waitress would be getting a good tip after all. She scraped her chair back, almost knocking it over in her haste to leave.

She was halfway to her feet when the man reached for her. In the next second he froze into immobility, restrained by Kit's hand around his throat. She sank back into the chair, her knees jelly, her heartbeat on pause.

"Take your hand off Kreestine and put your knife away." Kit's voice remained soft, strangely gentle. "I have no wish to hurt you."

The man blinked, seemingly unable to move, and Kit released him, smiling. "Good."

A round of laughter followed the man as he lurched out the door, one hand clapped to his throat.

"That's showin' him, Luke."

"Must be losin' your touch, boy. Or your nerve. Come on over and let ole Buck tell you how it's done."

"Drown it in a beer, Luke. Next round is on you."

Kristine barely heard the jeers through the nervous buzzing in her brain. Kit had done something to the man with his brief touch, and she wasn't at all sure she wanted to know what. "Let's get out of here."

"You haven't eaten your supper."

"I'm not hungry."

Kit noted the slight trembling of her hands and covered them with one of his own. "I am sworn to protect you, Kreestine. You will not come to harm."

"It's not me I'm worried about," she whispered, trying not to draw any more attention. "Let's just go, please, before somebody else decides to give you a haircut."

He laughed, about as inappropriate reaction as she could imagine, given the circumstances. "No one is going to cut my plait, *bahini*. Not even Sang Phala dared such a trespass in his later years, and he was compelled by convictions stronger than prejudice to use his razor on my head."

"Well, somebody dared at least once," she countered, glancing nervously around the bar and wishing he wouldn't argue. They were being watched, and none too kindly by her estimation.

"Yes," he said, grinning. "The Turk dared, but he was going for my throat and got my plait by mistake. Sometimes the gods are with us, eh?"

The man was too much, and Kristine was just the lady to tell him so. "You're in America now, Kit Carson, and we don't have nearly as many gods as you're used to," she informed him under her breath. "We only have one, and with everything else going on in the world tonight, He might be a little too busy to make sure you get out of this seedy bar in one piece. So why don't we do the smart thing and get out on our own while the getting is good? And while we're on the subject, if the damn thing causes you so much trouble, why don't you cut it off yourself?"

The barest flicker of anger lit the cinnamon depths of his eyes, giving her reason to regret the quickness of her tongue. "Do you not understand the importance of choice, Kreestine?"

"Yes. I do. I'm sorry," she said, shaking her head.

How long he wore his hair was none of her concern, and if it had been, she would have made no changes. Visions of her hands tangling in the thick auburn silk had infused her dreams with a sweet ache. When he'd held her so close in his room, the visions had resurfaced, sorely tempting her to touch, to pull away the chamois tie and let the strands slide through her fingers as she urged his mouth down to hers. "I'm leaving," she said abruptly. "You can do—"

"Then understand my choice," he interrupted, his hand wrapping around her wrist. "For six years the monks shaved my head. For six years it was the mark of my slavery. They beat all of us, but they beat me harder. My rice bowl was emptier, my days longer, my meditations never-ending, because I was no monk." He slowly rose to his feet, pulling her out of her chair, his gaze unflinching. "No more, Kreestine."

When he would have moved way, she stopped him by holding her arm steady. "I'm sorry."

He released her then, but his face remained devoid of emotion. "There is no reason for sorrow. I gained much in those years that other men spend a lifetime looking for and never find. Come." With his hand resting in the small of her back, he guided her out of the bar, and once again she found comfort in his touch.

The night had grown cool, the stars brighter. The moon had risen higher. The soft music of his steps played counterpoint to the crunch of gravel under their feet, but the tension in him remained. She'd had no right to be angry with him, Kristine told herself. They were supposed to be professionals working together, not two people wrapped up in a personal relationship she seemed incapable of controlling.

But everything about him affected her personally, very personally. She hadn't had a clear thought since he'd kissed her, a situation his non-kiss that evening had only magnified. She should have just kissed him and gotten it out of her system.

Oh, sure, Kristine, a mocking voice inside her head nagged at her. But she'd kissed Grant Thorp once and immediately decided not to subject either of them to any more boring dates.

She'd kissed Kit once, too, and his kiss had been so warm, so sweet. He had a way about him, a way of sharing his heat, a way of giving even as he took. She'd never felt anything quite as magically seductive as his mouth on hers, as his tongue tracing her lips and her teeth, seeking entrance. When he held her she didn't feel frigid; she went limp.

What would it be like, she wondered, to make love with a man who could read your mind?

Embarrassing? Probably, and she'd had enough embarrassment in her sex life.

Dangerous? Maybe, and she'd shown no inclination toward danger in her twenty-nine years on the planet. She'd made her share of snap judgments and rash decisions, but nothing approaching true danger, not even in her decisions concerning Kit.

Incredible.

The word floated across her mind as fact, without the doubt implied in a question, and a teasing warmth drifted up from her nerve endings to encompass her whole body.

"Wait," Kit said, stopping her by increasing the pressure of his hand against her back.

She glanced up at him, appalled by the direction she'd allowed her mind to wander, especially with him touching her. "It's nothing," she said quickly looking around for her car. "Nothing, really. I was just thinking about how warm it was in the bar and how—"

"Hush, *bahini.*" He slowly turned on the balls of his feet, searching the parking lot, and Kristine picked up on the undercurrent of unease in the air.

"What . . ." she started, but the question ended in hesitation. She hadn't noticed the other men leaving the bar, and now it was too late. They blocked a retreat back into the building, spreading in a haphazard circle between the cars and pickup trucks. Her first instinct was to back into something, and she did, into Kit. Her second instinct was to run, but she didn't, stayed by the command in his touch.

The shadowy figures wove in and out of the parked vehicles, and within moments her mouth was too dry to create anything more than a hoarse whisper. "Maybe we should make a run for the car."

"No, Kreestine." He turned her in his arms and placed a soothing kiss on her brow. "Do not run."

Well, now he'd confused her but good, she thought wildly, kissing her when she was all primed to panic. Her gaze darted from one hulking shadow to the next. There were five, four too many for a fair chance, and five too many to suit her. The very idea of a gang of subintelligent, bar-hopping cretins following them into a parking lot looking for trouble infuriated her. Kit couldn't fight all of them. "You can't fight all of them." And she couldn't fight one of them. "I think we should run. I—I never took any self-defense, and the last person I hit was much smaller than me. It was my little sister, actually, and about twenty years ago, and of course, she hit me back, and to tell you the truth I bruise rather easily, and—"

"Hush, Kreestine, there will be no fight."

He must know something she didn't, because it sure looked to her like those men meant business, fist kind of business. The five of them rounded the last layer of protective cars, trapping Kit and Kristine between two in front, three behind, and a pickup and a convertible on either side.

"Get in the car," Kit told her.

"It's not my car."

"I don't want you to get hurt."

"I *thought* you said there wasn't going to *be* a fight," she hissed. For some unknown reason she was not only furious with the cadre of jerks, she was angry at him again too. Men, she thought in disgust. It was always men. Not once in her life had she heard of a group of women piling out of a bar to duke it out in the parking lot. Not once.

"Obedience is a virtue, Kreestine, and one it would do you well to learn quickly."

"If'n you and your girlfriend wanna stop your confab," one of the men called, "we can get on with it, son. I've still got a mind for a souvenir." The man the others had called Luke pressed forward out of the trio on their right, his courage obviously revived by his buddies.

Kristine had heard enough. "I'm going to call the police."

"Police is not a good idea, Kreestine," Kit warned.

"You got that right, son," Luke said. "Hold on to her, Buck. Later we can show her a few things she can do with that mouth besides call the police." His crudity drew forth a round of laughter and a few, "Come on, Lukes" and sent a shot of startled terror through Kristine. A scream she had no intention of giving into lodged in her throat like a thick knot, making it nearly impossible to breathe. She would have run then and there except for Kit's calm, gentle voice cutting through the chuckling guffaws.

"The first man who touches her dies." His gaze drifted from one man to the next, one brow cocked in question. "Which of you is ready for your next life?" His confident words made them all pause, but only for a moment.

"Grab her, Buck."

"Dammit, Luke, grab her yourself if you're so hot."

Even Kristine felt the pressure in the dare. One of the cowboys walked away, muttering under his breath about a little fun getting out of hand.

Backed into a corner of his own making, Luke made a move forward, but only one. Kit caught Luke's fist with his palm, whipped him around, and slammed him against the door panel of the pickup.

That was it.

One of the other men knelt by Luke and made his diagnosis, "Out cold." Kit confirmed that conclusion when he, too, knelt down and checked Luke's pulse. He made a cursory examination of body parts and bones, his hands and demeanor as gentle as his voice had been.

Two others drifted away, and the fourth helped the first drag Luke to his feet.

Dear Lord, Kristine thought, still shaking. These people must be bored out of their ever-lovin' minds! She'd never considered herself the product of an overprotected childhood, but there were obviously some major gaps in her life that eight years of higher education hadn't filled in. She was shocked by her own naïveté and astounded by Kit's consideration of a man who'd insulted him and attempted to assault him.

"Come, Kreestine." Kit turned back to her and took her arm.

She jerked away, not trusting herself to speak.

He removed his hand and gestured toward her car, letting her lead the way with her long, stiff strides.

Kristine fought anger and incomprehensible tears as she ground the car through its gears up the mountain road. She'd never felt so helpless, so vulnerable, and she'd hated it. There should have been something she could have done, could have said, to diffuse the animosity and the stupidity behind it. But no, she'd stood there like a terrified female waiting for some man to do something to save her.

She tore into her driveway, slammed on the brakes, slammed out of the car, and slammed into her house. With each explosion of sound she heard the thud of a man's body hitting metal, all so he could have some fun. John Garraty was starting to look like a well-bred saint.

"It's best to let go of your anger, Kreestine."

She turned on him, unaware that he'd followed her into the house. "You *said* there wasn't going to be a fight!"

"That wasn't a fight."

"Well, what in the hell else do you call knocking somebody out cold?"

"Expedient."

"Expedient?" she blustered. "I would have thought someone with your background could have come up with something a little more *stylish* than beating a guy's *brains* out on a *truck door*!"

"The situation didn't call for style, and I barely touched him, Kreestine. I think he'd had too much to drink."

She stared at him, her mouth agape. "Too much to drink?"

He nodded sagely. "Yes. He'd had too much to drink and was feeling territorial. He obviously saw me as a threat to American womankind and decided violence was the answer. A poor choice, as always."

"Violence is a poor choice?" Her voice rose toward shrill. "This from a man who threatened to kill one of those overgrown idiots?"

"I would not have actually killed one of them," he said, stepping with her into the kitchen. "But under the circumstances I thought it wise to put the possibility in their minds."

Kristine watched him open the refrigerator and pull out a bottle of beer, an action that roused Mancos from his sleep in front of the fireplace. The mastiff padded over and stood by Kit, pressing his head against a jean-clad leg and waiting for a treat.

"Sha-sha, Mancos. Sha-sha."

Mancos let out a grumbly whine, but did as he

was told, passing his mistress in a dull dog daze to flop back down in the living room. Kristine didn't notice his change in loyalties. She was too busy working herself up again. Finally she could hold it no longer.

"You would have let them have me?"

Kit lowered his head against the refrigerator door and sighed, long and hard. She'd accomplished the impossible. She'd gotten under his skin, rattled the patience he'd spent years honing to a fine shield of composure. She'd made him angry.

He slowly turned to face her, forcing his voice to remain calm. He failed. "No, Kreestine. I would not have let them have you. I will not let anyone *have* you, not in the way they wished." He took a long draw off the beer, then set the bottle aside and started toward her. "Not now, not ever, because, *patni*"—he stopped in front of her and captured her face in his hands—"you are mine."

His mouth covered hers before she had time to think, and afterward she had no need to think, only desire for more of his kiss. She squeezed her hands into small fists, fighting the temptation to hold him, but temptation won. Her fingers trembled as she touched either side of his waist, and he slanted his mouth over hers again, pulling her higher, drawing her closer. She clutched at his tunic and felt the heat of his body spread through to her palms. Growing bolder, she slid her hands up his chest and traced the breadth of his shoulders. The strength of the muscles bunching in his arms made her feel weak and wanton, not helpless, not vulnerable, but waiting.

His low groan mingled with her sighs, and in

one powerful move he lifted her to the table top and pulled her snug against him, his hands splayed around her waist, his hips pressed between her thighs. Kristine began to melt from inside out, overwhelmed by the intensity of his passion. His mouth roamed from hers to the tender triangle where jaw met ear and neck, and she discovered a heretofore unknown erogenous zone. In truth, he was turning her whole body into an erogenous zone.

She tilted her head to taste the nape of his neck, but his hand cupped her chin, stopping her.

"Don't," he whispered into her ear, and kissed her again. "Unless you are willing to come to my bed." Another kiss followed the last, lower on her neck, gliding down to the curve of her collarbone. His braid slid over his shoulder, so close to her hand. "Will you come, Kreestine?"

Yes . . .

"Good." He moved to gather her in his arms, and a cold dose of reality splashed into her fantasy.

"No! I mean . . . no. We hardly know each other. We've barely met. I can't just fall into bed with—with you." Her voice softened in dismay. She didn't know what to think anymore.

"Ah, then you only want to play at love." He kissed the corners of her mouth, teasing her with his tongue, and a bold hand slid up to caress her breast. "I like to play, too, Kreestine, but—" He paused to graze her lower lip with his teeth." I'm quickly losing patience with the game. Come to me when you are ready."

He kissed her once more, a lingering exploration of her mouth she couldn't resist. When he pulled away she found his braid sliding through the hand she'd wrapped around it in an attempt to hold him longer and closer.

Thoroughly embarrassed by the betraying action, she released the plait and lowered her gaze only to have her blush heighten. She watched his large, rough hand slide slowly up her body, leaving a trail of heat along her thigh, over her belly, her breasts, and up to her throat. The tips of his fingers tilted her chin until she was looking at him.

He was smiling, his eyes dark with a slumber to match his voice. "It's a good game, though, Kreestine. A very good game."

Seven

He was crazy. She was crazy. The whole world had gone crazy.

Kristine pulled more papers out of the office waste-baskets, muttering silently to herself. Pencil shavings dusted her knees, making grimy lead stains on her blue-and-white-striped jeans. She'd already spilled coffee on the matching T-shirt, and the sun hadn't even come up yet.

Without including her workplace, the office was immaculately organized, thanks to Kit, but she more than made up for his tidiness with her small area of intense clutter. The man was obsessed with order. She bet he'd never lost anything in his life—until he'd met her.

"Dammit." She upended the wastebasket and gave it a shake. He'd entrusted her with this breakdown lists of the trunks he'd dismantled on Saturday, but with little else concerning the *Kāh-gyur*. She had typed three of the handwritten lists into her computer, but the fourth had disappeared.

Her mustard-yellow blouse fluttered out of the bottom of the wastebasket, and she sat back on her heels and covered her face with her hands. She wished she'd burned the damn thing. She wouldn't cry. She never cried. Crying would get her nowhere.

She'd kept out of his way all day yesterday, speaking only when spoken to, maintaining her veneer of professionalism at the cost of her nerves and her sleep. He'd worked in the garage taking apart the trunks, identifying each printing block and taking a partial rubbing, numbering the pieces and wrapping them for storage, and making the lists he'd then given to her for safekeeping. He hadn't asked for her help, and she hadn't found the courage or the confidence to go to this room and offer it.

What was wrong with her? More prestige than she'd ever dared to hope for was within her reach, and all she could think about was the man who had brought the opportunity to her. He was more than unorthodox. He was a law unto himself. Anyone else would have been crushed by the responsibility he'd taken on, with his daring escapade and flight into exile. She'd awakened twice in the night, once in a cold sweat of fear, worrying over the garage catching fire, or a freak tornado whirling out of the sky and sucking up the *Kāh-gyur,* and she'd called herself a fool for getting tangled up with his forbidden treasure. The second time she'd awakened, she hadn't known what to call herself except overheated, overimaginative, and thoroughly frustrated.

Had he put a spell on her? Her every thought turned to him. Kit Carson had become the bane of her existence. She didn't know him, didn't understand him, had never met anyone even remotely similar to him in looks or temperament. His mind worked in unknown ways, and it worked on her. She was fascinated by him, purely and simply fascinated. She understood her infatuation with John Garraty. He'd been everything she wanted to be: well known in his field, respected, intellectual, tenured.

Kit Carson was well known, but the rest was up for grabs. He wasn't at all the kind of man she would have chosen for herself. He was civilized only to a degree, and that degree in another culture; more sensual than intellectual, yet highly intelligent in ways she couldn't begin to comprehend.

But then, she'd chosen John Garraty with all his tenure and respectability, and had done nothing but regret the choice ever since. Maybe she didn't know what was good for her. For a moment, just a moment, when she'd awakened for the second time in the middle of the night, she'd thought the only thing that could save her and give her peace was climbing the stairs to Kit's room and rediscovering the sheer wonder of his kisses.

A muffled groan caught in her throat, and she dropped her hands to her thighs. Damn him. When he put a thought into a person's head, he really knew how to make it stick.

Come to me when you are ready. The arrogance alone in the remark should have been enough to turn her off. Instead, it had created the exact opposite effect.

She looked down at the rubble piled around her on the floor. The list had been there. *The* Lois Shepherd and *the* Thomas Stein were coming to her house tomorrow, and she and Kit had to be ready. If she screwed up the deal, he might never leave.

Crazy, she thought again, slapping her hand over her face. She was going crazy. A thirteenth-century antiquity was slowly being dismantled in her garage and all she could relate it to was the man who'd brought it. What had happened to her sense of history? Her career goals? Her life?

Her hand slid down from her eyes to cover her mouth, and she spotted it, a pale green piece of paper from his journals lying her desk. She almost collapsed in relief.

Kit laid a white piece of paper over the eighty-eighth printing block and ran a two-inch square of charcoal down one side. He numbered the paper with a fine-point pen, then marked the blank side with his ink brush, stroking the ancient Mongolian characters into place.

He'd worked throughout the cold night. Sleep had proved to be more labor than rest. He'd waited as he had the previous night for Kristine to come to him, and he would wait longer, until their time ran out.

He set the cotton-bond paper aside and picked up a sheet of rice paper. He took greater care with the second, complete rubbing, for these were his to keep, decipher, and study. For him the words held more importance than the wooden blocks used to make them. When the ink dried on the first piece of paper, he filed it for Shepherd and Stein, who would be arriving the next day, then slid another brass bead on his abacus to the right.

What did she want? What did she need from him? The day he'd spent with her had been enlightening, but not in the manner of his youthful enlightenments.

What did he want from her? He'd called her *patni*, wife, without forethought. Was there meaning in this? he wondered. Sang Phala would have said yes, all of life was rich with meaning, but his second father had passed beyond his reach into the nothingness of Nirvana.

A wave of loneliness washed through his mind, forcing his eyes closed. Jealousy and loneliness. What other surprises did she have in store for him? The monastery had been a haven from the crueler emotions, providing a spiritual oneness against the emptiness he now felt so far from his home.

Patni. Half of a whole, yin to yang. He'd left the monks in search of his manhood and the life he'd been born to live, rebelling against the life his father's death and Sang Phala's promise had thrust upon him. For the past fifteen years, since he'd run from the monastery, he had lived with his convictions of freedom tempered by his own conscience, only to reach this place and this time where he was suddenly half of a whole. She was working mysterious magic on him.

He laid his brush aside and sighed. Work was no balm for his distraction. Desire had grown beyond want. He needed Kristine Richards, a very stubborn, creatively haphazard American woman with more ambition than sense. Wanting to make love with her did not surprise him. Wanting to make a life with her did. He had plans she didn't fit into.

He'd slipped out of Asia like a thief in the night, two steps in front of the internationally recognized law of the Chinese and one step ahead of the Turk, stealing away with a hundred-odd pounds of ancient wood holding the translated words of Buddha. He'd done it as a gesture of faith and, he admitted, because no one had thought he'd find it, let alone get away with it. He'd traded the last of his reputation for his adopted people and his pride. He had no regrets, but neither did he plan on remaining in exile for the rest of this life.

He needed to place the *Kāh-gyur* safely to put it forever out of the Turk's reach. He needed to publish his research and regain his legitimate standing. He needed to bide his time, until the storm of threats and recriminations died away. Then he'd go back to the Chinese. He'd go to them and promise them anything if they'd let him back into Tibet.

He needed to return, for many reasons. He'd been born in the frozen wastelands of "the roof of the world," and the stark purity of its light and the solitude it offered were ingrained in his soul.

But what was solitude to a lonely man? And was the sunlight of the high Himalayas any purer than what he saw in Kristine's eyes?

Questions, he thought, slowly rising from the floor. Questions were so easy to come by. The temporal world whirled on its axis in a flood of questions, drawing fools and mortals in its wake. He was both, for the answers he sought lay not in his heart and mind, but in Kristine.

He had vowed to protect her from all things,

except himself and the unexpected love he felt growing deep inside. Why couldn't she have been a concubine? Mere lust was easy to conquer. Love, it seemed, could only be surrendered to.

The first light of day rimmed his windowsill, then spilled into the room and spread across the floor. He followed the path of sunshine with a quiet, barefoot tread to look down on the house where she dwelled. Was she sleeping? Were her dreams as troubled as his? Did she understand better than he the forces drawing them together?

Questions. More questions. Weariness bowed his head, and his loneliness grew.

Kristine squeezed another dollop of cheese spread on another tiny cracker. Her house was clean by anyone's standards, even her mother's; Mancos was chained in the backyard, for everyone's peace of mind; and her third batch of canapés looked better than the first, which she'd consigned to the garbage disposal. White wine cooled in her refrigerator. A fresh pot of coffee brewed on the counter. She had mints, napkins, ashtrays, coasters, and fancy nuts.

A quick glance at her kitchen clock proved all of her worst fears. Shepherd and Stein would appear at any minute, and Kit Carson was almost out of her life. The two events were inextricably bound.

With an unsteady hand, she placed a ring of olive on top of each cracker, giving it a little push into the cheese. The last thing she needed was self-destructing canapés. She'd never hosted anything as monumental as the auctioning off of a rare antiquity. Her nerves and her pulse were in a dead heat for the quarter-mile-speed record. Sleep was a memory, and she knew that every tossing-and-turning hour was beaten into the bags under her eyes. She'd tried concealer. She'd tried base, mascara, and eyeliner, and she'd wiped it all off twice, opting instead for huge earrings as her major distraction.

"Kreestine?"

She jumped at the sound of his voice, bumping her head on an open cupboard door. She pretended she hadn't and pushed another olive ring into the cheese. "What?"

The sharpness of her question sparked an instant flare of anger in Kit. He tamped it down with the force of his will, and was amazed at just how much force and how much will it took to accomplish what had always been an inherently natural act. He was not pleased either with the deterioration of their relationship. He'd left her alone too long to suit him and obviously too long to suit her.

She wore her hair up again, in a style he hadn't seen. A wide gold clip arced up the back of her head, turning her piles of hair into a cascade of ebony curls. Large, delicate gold earrings, studded with red jewels, hung halfway down her neck, the first jewelry he'd seen her wear. He liked the exoticness of them, the tinkling sound they made when she turned her head. He liked the soft red heavy cotton shirt she wore. It flowed in a single unadorned piece to the middle of her thighs, and matched her skintight, ankle-length pants of the same color and fabric. In his country, he would have had to hide her away in those pants. He liked the bareness of her feet. He did not like the smudges of weariness beneath her eyes.

"All this is not necessary," he said, gesturing at the trays of canapés and the sparkling glasses lining the counter.

Typical, Kristine thought, her mouth tightening. She'd slaved the morning away making everything nearly perfect for his guests, and he had the gall to tell her it wasn't necessary. What was she supposed to have done? Invited Lois Shepherd and Thomas Stein into her home, then popped the tops off a couple of bottles of beer? Men didn't understand anything.

"But it is very gracious," he added. "Loe-eese and Thomas will feel welcomed."

"Thank you," she said, shoving olives onto crackers, not the least bit mollified by his politeness.

"I am grateful," he said.

"You're welcome." A bit too much strength mashed her last olive ring and broke the cracker beneath. "Dammit." She tossed the ruined canapé into the sink and set about rearranging the tray. Now it would never match the one sitting in the refrigerator. "Dammit," she said again. She wanted everything perfect, organized down to the last damn cracker. She had a point to prove to herself.

"It's just a cracker, Kreestine," he reassured her.

"No. No, you're wrong," she said, her voice strained. "It was more than a cracker." Arranging with one hand, she reached with the other hand and opened the refrigerator door. She'd have to throw away one of the other canapés in order to get everything right. In the split second of distraction she heard a telltale crunch.

Whirling around, she caught him licking his fingers.

"Good," he said, offering her a smile.

It was too much. She'd fallen in love with a heartless barbarian who had no conception of the social graces required to host visiting dignitaries, or of the importance of symmetrical canapé trays. Tears she refused to let fall welled in her eyes, her tired, bloodshot, dark-rimmed eyes.

He reached up to caress her cheek, and his voice was soft with contrition. "What's this, *patni*?"

"Don't call me that, please." She'd looked the word up and knew what it meant. Wife. She wasn't his wife. She would never be his wife. He was too alive, too sexually male, too wild, too different, too everything, and she wasn't enough of anything, least of all enough of a woman to please him. She tried to brush his hand away, but he captured her fingers with his own.

"In this you are wrong, Kreestine."

Lord help her. All she wanted to do was die.

"And this I will not allow."

"Stop it," she moaned, mortified. She tried to pull away, but this, it seemed, was another thing he would not allow. His other hand slid to the back of her neck and closed in a gentle fist around her hair, tilting her head back and forcing her to meet his gaze. His eyes, lit with a dark fire, were shot through with gold and russet, and rich, sensual mysteries.

He guided her arm behind her back and forced her closer, entwining his fingers with hers and holding her hand at the base of her spine, taking complete control and leaving her helpless to resist.

"When we join, *patni*, we will both know the truth of which I speak." His voice was a husky drawl, his lilt muted by the intensity of emotion.

"Already I feel the warmth of your desire and the heat of your need matching mine."

She felt the heat, too, waves of it like wind-fanned flames, and if he didn't kiss her, she *would* die.

He saved her with the barest brushing of his mouth over hers, teasing her to the point of agony and pushing her beyond the barrier of past humiliation. She stretched up on tiptoe, wanting him, nipping at his mouth. He took her, sliding his tongue down the length of hers and filling her with slow, licking flames of molten passion.

She groaned and he held her tighter, intoxicating her with his erotic duel. Canapés disappeared from her thoughts, along with the kitchen around her, the floor she stood on, and the very air she breathed. All of her awareness focused on him and the sensations he created, emotional and physical. His body hardened against her, his arms tightened, flexing around her with power and strength, even as he freed her captured hand.

She found good use for it, tunneling her fingers into the auburn silk framing his face. She traced the curve of his cheekbones with her thumbs and discovered the delight of touching his lips as he kissed her. A soft bite proved he liked her hands there, and when she slid them lower, down the front of his chest, his low groan proved he liked her hands anywhere as long as they were on him.

Ah, woman, he said silently, willing her to feel his thoughts the way he felt hers, *you are a welcoming softness in my arms. Your taste is sweet, your scent is lush with the perfume of arousal. Let me . . . let me . . .*

Yes.

His answer to hers was the sound of his heavy belt hitting the floor. He swept her up into his arms, and this time she offered no protest.

"You have agreed?" he asked, carrying her across the living room. When she didn't reply, he stopped with one booted foot on the lowest stair and kissed her again, his teeth grazing her lips, his tongue plunging inside her mouth, enticing her into submission. The long, deep strokes were unnecessary, but too pleasurable to stop. She met each one with a sigh, and Kit felt those sighs like a slow pull on his loins.

"You have agreed," he growled, breaking the kiss and continuing up the stairs to her bedroom. He would take her there, among the white lace and pillows, the frills of woman's things. Later that night she would sleep with him wrapped in the warmth of his arms and his blankets and robes, and he would take her again.

He lowered her to the bed, then followed her down into the disarray of cotton sheets and satin comforters, inhaling her lingering scent on the fabric and nuzzling his face into the crook of her neck, finding there the headier pleasures of the woman herself.

His mouth glided across her skin, tasting, leaving a trail of irresistible, wet warmth. She wanted his mouth again on hers.

The desire no sooner blossomed in her mind than it was fulfilled with urgency and passion, his firm lips stealing the need and answering the yearning, and bringing upon her an even greater yearning. The pressure of his weight upon her, of his thigh pressing up between her legs, did crazy things to her thoughts. She instinctively lifted her hips higher.

Kit slipped a hand beneath her, holding her there, and slowly raised his head. A languorous smile played about his mouth, and he increased the pressure ever so slightly, rubbing against her.

"This is a very good game, eh?" One brow lifted in knowing confirmation as she gasped. Fully clothed, he made her feel things she'd only ready about—and then he began to remove his clothes.

On his knees above her, straddling her hips, he unbuttoned the first few buttons on his black tunic, then pulled the shirt over his head. Muscle moved beneath his dark skin, smooth and graceful, rippling in a rhythm to match his every movement and making her long to touch him.

"This you shall do, *patni*, in many ways," he assured her, pulling her upright. In one smooth, fluid motion, he slipped her long shirt off, removing the clip from her hair in the same gesture. It was magic, it had to be, but no more so than the look in his eyes when he saw what she wore beneath.

Her dark hair slid over her creamy white shoulders and the soft, heavy curves of her breasts cupped in red lace, and the knot of desire in his belly tightened. He had not expected red lace, not on Kristine.

He lifted his gaze to her eyes and knew the only teasing he dared was with his mouth. She wanted him, but was unsure of the path. The uncertainty bound her to him in yet another way. He wanted her, too, but first he needed to erase all of her doubts. When he took her, it would be as he'd promised, with her own fire matching his, with her own need pulling him farther than she'd been before.

Delicately, he traced the edge of the lace with his fingers, and he let all the wonder he felt fill his voice with tenderness. "There is much love in my heart for you, Kreestine," he murmured, easing her back on the bed. He lowered his mouth to her breast and lost himself in the erotic sensation of tasting her softness through the barrier of red lace.

Soon that barrier became too much, and with another skilled movement he left her wondering about a Far Eastern barbarian's understanding of the workings of Western lingerie. Her bra joined the pile of clothes building on the floor, piece by incredible piece. His mouth trailed over her, leaving gentle love bits on her skin. His hands followed with tantalizing caresses, until she had no choice but to touch him in turn.

His body was like satin and steel, hard and so very alive, and soft on the tips of her fingers, so warm. The heat of him invaded her on every level of feeling, from the sentient layer of her skin to the hidden corners of her mind. He took the dark coldness of her doubts and filled them with light and drugging sensation. Her senses pooled wherever he seared her with his mouth, making her believe each place was where she needed him most, until he moved to the next, and the next.

This time, when she tilted her head and rubbed her mouth against his skin, he let her taste. Her teeth grazed his jaw, lightly, with just enough force to let him know she was there. She rolled with him when he removed her leggings, thinking only of retracing the path with her tongue and returning to the hot, sweet magic of his mouth. With just his kiss he gave her more pleasure than she'd ever known, for his kiss demanded everything from her and returned it all twofold.

Willingly, she fell deeper under the spell he wove, moving to the gentle commands she felt and marveling at his responses to her. Her every caress heightened his arousal, giving her the power he relinquished and sweeping her higher and higher. He laved the satin softness of her inner thigh with his tongue, then went farther, teaching her things no monk had ever imagined. She gasped, and he relented, but only long enough to reach her bare breasts and start the spiral of desire anew.

He was masculinity personified at its gentlest and most invincible, an erotically fascinating mix of carefully controlled physical strength and unleashed emotions. He gave her the best of both, inciting her mind with the visual clarity of his most sensuous thoughts and inducing a fever of need in her body. He touched her in places and in ways she'd never dreamed of until he'd given her the dream in her mind.

With the quiet insistence of his thoughts he told her what he wanted. With the guidance of his hands he taught her the moves. When she hesitated, he urged her on. When she complied, he whispered words of satisfaction in her ear, his voice rough with the depth of his pleasure.

"Ah, Kreestine . . . Kreestine . . ." He stiffened above her, his breathing unsteady. He'd played the game too long; she'd learned too quickly. She caressed him again, her hand slipping between the gaping opening of his pants, and doing only what he'd asked, but it was too much. Against his wishes, he found himself pressing into her palm, his thoughts chaotically focused on one driving need—to be inside her.

The picture of his need was clear in her mind, shimmering in waves of heat and the sensation he promised her. With his smoldering gaze he forced her to hold the thought, living with him the loving to come. His hands were sure and quick as he stood up and took off his jeans, and never once did he let her lose sight of what he wanted, what he would have—her melting over him, tightening around him. The heat built and built inside her, fueled by his desires and her understanding, until she closed her eyes and moaned.

He covered her then, lowering himself onto her, pressing her deeper into the bed, and slowly, ever so slowly, sheathing himself in her white fire. Moment by moment he replaced the vivid fantasy with the hard reality of his body, capturing the soft sounds of her pleasure with his mouth. The game was over, banished by the ache he strove to ease. Yet he wanted the easing to last forever.

Kristine tunneled her hands through his hair, releasing his plait and dragging her fingers down the length of auburn silk. She kissed him. From the very bottom of her soul she kissed him. His skin grew slick beneath her hands, dampened by the exertion of his flexing muscles, his power, the strain of his control. She welcomed the weight of him, the exquisite pressure of each stroke, the friction, the scent of him, the strength.

Kit filled her endlessly, again and again, physically losing himself inside of her and mentally waiting, waiting for her search to bring her closer to the elusive fountainhead of consummation. He thrust deeply and groaned at the pleasure coursing up his spine. The waiting could not last much longer. He sucked her tongue into his mouth and slid his hand between their bodies, giving her what she sought.

Ah, woman, woman, what you do to me, what you give . . . These things I have not known before. Take of me, Kreestine. Take everything and still I will find more to give, for you are the one . . . the only one . . .

She gasped, her breathing stopped, her body stilled at the potent sensations ripping through her; and suddenly he was the one taking, taking the shuddering power of her climax and using it for his own. He surged into her for the last time and released himself in concert with the rapt pleasure consuming her.

In the gentle aftermath, they lay in each other's arms. Visually, Kristine traced the curves of muscle in his chest and the taut plane of his abdomen, down to where her hand rested, slender and pale against his darker skin and the soft auburn hair disappearing beneath the sheet. She gently raked her nails through the enticing pelt and felt the strong arm around her waist tighten and draw her closer.

She glanced up and caught the hint of a smile playing about his mouth. His eyes slowly opened, capturing her. He raised his head off the pillow and teased his mouth over the upper curve of her breast.

"I have not seen skin such as this, Kreestine, like cream on my lips and sugar on my tongue. You are very beautiful . . . very beautiful. And you are mine." His other hand came into play, sliding up her thigh, his bracelets chiming together and making the music she heard in her heart. A long hank of hair fell over his shoulder and down his arm.

Lord, what had she done? She wondered at the serenity she felt in his arms, at the desire rising within her to touch him, to spread her hand through his thick hair and bare the column of his throat for her kiss. No monk he. Kautilya Carson had been made for love, for loving a woman senseless. Every beautiful line of him begged for her touch, and she longed to feel again his hardness and strength. He'd taken her outside herself, and in the taking had bound her to him.

Her fingers tightened on his wrist as he cupped her breast, to hold him there, not to push him away. The knowledge he'd given her made it impossible to push him away. He offered too much pleasure. She lowered her head and pressed her lips to his temple, wondering at how she was so easily addicted to the taste of him and the warmth of his response. Here was the man she'd never dreamed of, the man she couldn't have imagined, and he was in her arms, teaching her once more of his ways.

She surrendered herself to him in the second mating, knowing it was more than pleasure he gave, more than pleasure he took. Awkwardness turned to grace under his caresses, shyness to boldness, and through it all, an outlaw slowly turned into her heart's love.

Eight

She couldn't take her eyes off him. She didn't want to take her eyes off him. Shepherd and Stein had been thankfully late, wandering for over two hours amidst the unmarked, unpaved roads on the hill. Two hours burned into Kristine's memory with all the passion she and Kit had shared.

She watched, mesmerized, as he tapped his pouch of tobacco into the paper bent between his fingers. She remembered every touch of his hands. He lifted the paper to his mouth and glided his tongue across one edge, his eyes meeting hers across the distance of the coffee table. She blushed but held his gaze, reliving for a moment the memories reflected in his eyes.

"Remarkable," Thomas Stein murmured, looking through a magnifying glass at one of the wooden printing blocks Kit had laid out for their perusal. Thomas was the older of the two curators, his salt-and-pepper hair ringing a bald spot he didn't attempt to conceal. His gray pinstriped suit was immaculately tailored. "Absolutely remarkable," he repeated.

Kit grinned, and Kristine's blush increased, but still she couldn't tear her gaze away from him. He knew what he'd done to her, and she couldn't forget, not even with other people in the room.

"Amazing," Lois Shepherd agreed. She stood over by the carefully packed storage boxes Kit had carried from the garage to the living room, tallying them. She was crisp and neat in a navy gabardine suit and white blouse with matching spectator heels, the epitome of cool professionalism.

From here on out the *Kāh-gyur* would be handled with the awe and respect it deserved, and handled by Kristine. Kit had made his wishes clear in that respect, letting both curators know that all test results and specialist reports were to pass through her hands before any others. They had balked at first, but Kit had insisted, and they all knew who held the winning hand in this particular game.

Kit rolled the cigarette between his thumb and forefinger, then struck a match with his other hand, content beyond measure with the day and what he'd found deep inside Kristine. She had filled him with wonder, made all the choices of his past the right ones, for following their paths had brought him to her.

He drew deeply on the cigarette and leaned forward, resting his forearms on his thighs. Still smiling, he blew a smoke ring across the room and watched in satisfaction as it settled around her wineglass and wrist, drawing her amazed gaze back to his eyes.

"Have you stabilized them?" Thomas asked, still peering through his glass.

"We spent three days at Narthang having them blessed and wrapped for the journey," Kit said, as if that explained the *Kāh-gyur*'s good condition.

"Nothing more?" Thomas asked, raising a doubtful gaze.

Kit's smile broadened. "And some temporary first-aid. PVA on the front where necessary. PEG Four Thousand, fungicide, and ethanol on the back. Your lab shouldn't have any trouble reversing the treatment."

"They traveled remarkably well," Thomas said, choosing another printing block for inspection.

"Have you translated them?" Lois asked. "Do you know what section of the *Tripitaka* we have?"

"One hundred and forty-two nonconsecutive pages of the Discipline, the mystical antidote for the original sin of lust, *Rāga*." Kit answered Lois, but his gaze lingered on Kristine.

If there were an underlying irony in his tone, Kristine chose to ignore it. She hadn't even known what lust was until he'd taught her the craving. Her skin burned wherever his gaze settled, melting her hard-won composure. She only prayed Lois and Thomas couldn't feel the heat filling the room. Sang Phala must truly have had his hands full with his bartered-for renegade. A good portion of the power she had felt from their first encounter, she now realized, was pure sexual energy.

"Well, it's amazing," Lois said.

Yes. The thought drifted from Kristine's mind, cast forth with an unconscious sigh.

Ah, yes, Kristine. You are sweetness incarnate in my arms. His smile faded and his eyes darkened, and he slowly shook his head with the same wonderment she felt.

"No?" Lois's voice broke into their silent communication. "Then we've got a major problem. You should have told me on the phone, Kit, and saved me a trip."

"Told you what, Lo-eese?" He glanced up, realizing he'd missed a part of the conversation. At least part of the less important conversation swirling through the living room.

Lois stepped back from the boxes. "I can't touch this stuff without some kind of authorization from somebody. You knew that before you left." She took another step. "You promised—"

"And I never break a promise," Kit interrupted her, reaching into his breast pocket and pulling out a sealed envelope. He rose from the couch and handed it to Lois.

Thomas stood up and walked over to his compatriot, waiting while she broke the seal. Together they read the document, and two pairs of eyebrows rose in unison.

"Did you really meet him?" Lois asked, scanning the paper again.

"I accepted it from the god-king's own hand," Kit answered. "The Dalai Lama has little recourse against the imperialistic tendencies of his northern neighbor, but he is still the spiritual leader of his people. The *Kāh-gyur*, we both agreed, is a very spiritual asset."

Lois nodded. "I'm satisfied."

Thomas balked. "It's still contraband."

"Back out if you want to, Stein," Lois said. "L.A. will take full responsibility and all one hundred and forty-two blocks. I've had an international law team on this from the beginning. They've been looking for a loophole in the antiquities law"—she glanced at Kit—"and I think our friend has delivered the key."

Thomas still wasn't convinced. "It's a long shot."

Lois looked at him over the rims of her wire-framed glasses. "Then leave before we get down to business."

The older man held his ground, though none too confidently. "Chicago has lawyers too."

"I've heard a rumor to that effect," Lois drawled, baiting the man.

"I'm in, Shepherd," Thomas grumbled, taking a white handkerchief out of his pocket and dabbing at his brow. "I'm in."

"Good." Lois turned her attention to Kit, giving Kristine a nod on the way. "I think everybody in this room knows that what we're dealing with here is priceless, but those of us who have dealt with Mr. Carson in the past also know he has never failed to set a price for his services." She tapped her glasses farther down on her nose and narrowed her gaze at Kit. "Usually an outrageous price."

"I have lost much in this deal already, Lo-eese." Kit took a deep draw of smoke, then leaned forward to crush the cigarette in an ashtray.

"Such as?" Lois asked in a wary tone.

"My homeland, my house, most of my possessions, a yak and a mule, and a good portion of my freedom."

"You're Buddhist, Kit," Lois reminded him. "You know freedom is a state of mind. Nepal is not for sale, so I don't see that entering into the bargain, but I have connections in Kathmandu. I could arrange for the sale of your house and to have your possessions shipped over here, and I'll split the difference on the livestock."

"No." He stood up, and with his familiar musical grace, walked over to the large windows framing the reservoir. Three pairs of eyes followed his every step, two pairs with caution, and one pair, the hue of mountain violets, with utter fascination at the beauty of his movement. Kristine knew whatever spell he'd started with his first kiss had been sealed in the room above them.

He rested his hand high on the window frame, and a cascade of gold slid down his arm. They waited. Finally he spoke, and when he did, all their gazes held the same reaction—disbelief.

"I want to go home." The lilt of his accent was softened by the true need that infused his words.

"Unlikely," Thomas said.

"It's your head." Lois said, then shrugged. "I'll do what I can."

Kristine had no such comment to offer. Home? Away from her? After he'd stolen her heart? And in record time. She reached for her wineglass and found her trembling fingers couldn't hold the stem. She pulled her hand back into her lap.

"What's your price on the *Kāh-gyur*?" Lois asked.

"Four hundred thousand."

"Four hundred thousand what? Rupees?" The older woman didn't even attempt to hide her shock.

"No, Lo-eese." He turned to face the curator. "The hard currency of American dollars."

Thomas sank onto the couch, but Lois quickly recovered. Kristine wasn't even close to recovering.

"One hundred thousand, and I'll buy the mule and the yak," Lois said.

"One of my muleteers was injured. I need to compensate his family for his lost labor. Three hundred and fifty thousand, and two hundred dollars apiece for the animals."

"That's a damned expensive yak, Kit. I'll give you fifty for the mule, and know I've been robbed, and one hundred for the yak, not a penny more. One hundred and seventy-five thousand.

"Three."

"Two. Bottom line."

"You'll arrange for the trust?" he asked.

She nodded. "What's your commission?"

"Fifty percent."

"Your neck is coming pretty high these days, isn't it?"

A rogue's smile teased his mouth, and he lifted one broad shoulder in a nonchalant shrug. "Such are the economics of risk."

The economics of risk, Kristine repeated silently, wrapping her hands tighter around each other. Now why in the hell hadn't she thought of that before she'd fallen in love with him? The outlaw was going to break her heart.

"I'm catching the red-eye back to Los Angeles," Lois said, "and I've got a crew waiting in Denver to pack this thing right. Unless, of course, you want to chant over it a few more times and save me the trouble?"

Kit laughed and drew the older woman into a hug. "For you, Lo-eese, I will chant."

And what was he willing to do for her? Kristine wondered. Love her and leave her?

The afternoon slid into dusk and then into evening with every minute feeling like her last. She pored over her computerized versions of his journals and his catalog of artifacts, explaining her work and the system Kit had used to Lois and Thomas. She had voluminous packages for both of them, and both expressed an interest in the university's project. Lois even offered to write an introduction to her book on the temples and shrines of Tibet. Dean Chambers, indeed, would be impressed, Kristine thought, and Harry would probably never forgive himself.

It was as close to acclaim as Kristine had ever gotten. She held the opportunity dear, knowing it might be the only thing left after he was gone, a published work of historical significance and the shadowed glory of being the conduit of knowledge of Chatren-Ma. It wasn't enough.

Damn him. Who did he think he was, to waltz into her life and waltz back out? Dear Lord, had she really made love with him? She lifted her gaze over Lois's shoulder and watched him go over the boxes with Thomas, double-checking the inventory lists.

Had she really held him in her arms and felt the very life of him surround, invade, and fill her with the sweetest love she'd ever known? Had she really kissed him with desperate need, wanting nothing more than to know the heat of him forever? Had she tangled her fingers in his hair and pulled him down to her again and again, turning ravenous for every touch of his mouth.

Yes, her memories answered as her gaze drifted up his long, jean-clad legs and over his broad back and shoulders to the profiled angle of his jaw. His bracelets, those broad bands of gold incised with the fauna of the high plateaus—snow leopard and ram, a coiled panther striking down a stag, the gentler symbolism of birds nesting in trees—jangled when he knelt on the floor and lifted the bottom of one box for Thomas to notate a number in his book. She followed the path of his plait down between his shoulder blades, then at last returned her gaze to the folio Lois was studying.

Yes, she'd made love with him, and she knew she'd never be free of the whispers he'd put in her mind, of the imprint of his body, the touch he gave that went beyond both.

The older woman sifted through the papers and shuffled around through a couple more notebooks, her brow furrowing.

"Is something wrong?" Kristine asked, forcing her attention back to the job at hand.

"I've known him a long time, Kristine," Lois said absently, continuing her search, "since before Lishan. He's not like most men, but then neither was his father."

The personal turn of the conversation surprised her, but she couldn't help but follow Lois's lead. "Which father do you mean?"

Curious, brown eyes peered at her over the rim of Lois's glasses, and Kristine thought she detected a note of surprise in the older woman's expression. "He told you about Sang Phala?"

Kristine eased down into one of the kitchen-table chairs, her own curiosity at full flame. "Only that Sang Phala was the one who took him into the monastery."

"Kicking and screaming by all accounts," Lois said after pausing to remove her glasses. In those short moments Kristine knew she'd been scrutinized inside out, upside down, and backward by an expert. "He was nine when Sang Phala found him with the Khampas. By then Kit was wilder than a cub wolf, rebellious, resentful, confused, and still too young to understand why he'd been abandoned by his parents."

"Abandoned?" Kristine was hanging on every word, every bit of information about the unique man who'd slipped inside her defenses, but she hadn't expected that particular word.

"They died, but to a child it's the same," Lois explained. "He'd been left alone. I looked for him myself. Melanie and Dwayne were both good friends of mine."

Melanie, Kristine thought, testing the name in her mind. His mother's name had been Melanie.

"But you couldn't find him?" she prompted, not wanting the discussion to end. No other explanation made sense, but Lois quickly dissuaded her.

"Oh, I found him all right." Lois shifted one of the folders on top of another. "And I had the legal right to bring him back to the United States. He was, and is, an American citizen."

Kristine heard the regret in the older woman's voice and wondered what could have compelled her to leave her friend's son in such a wild land.

Lois glanced up at Kit. "I chose to leave him in the monastery." Then, as if seeking confirmation of her decision, she said, "Look at him, Kristine. Can you imagine him different than he is? In a Brooks Brothers suit?"

No. Try as she might, Kristine couldn't fit those shoulders into pinstripes. She couldn't fit his smile behind a facade of civilization. He was elemental, of the earth and sky, and no outward trappings could enhance the man he'd become.

"He was still hurting so badly when I found

him," Lois continued, sounding lost in her own thoughts. "A little boy shoved from an extreme of freedom into an extreme of discipline. I couldn't turn his world upside-down again. I wasn't sure I could offer him the peace Sang Phala promised me would be his." A fleeting smile graced the curator's mouth. "I could have wrung the old man's neck when I found out Kit had run away. Those were the bad years, not knowing where he was, not knowing if he was dead or alive, wondering how he'd survive on his own. Then the kid shows up at Lishan, and the rest, as they say, is history."

She sighed, her gaze returning to the pile of folders. "For a moment, when I found him in the monastery, when I stood in the cold hallway watching his small head bowed in prayers, that tinge of red hair like a beacon among so much darkness, I thought he could be mine, that I could bring him home and raise him as my son." Lois lifted her head and gave Kristine a long, thoughtful look, and her voice softened. "But he never belonged to me, Kristine. He's never belonged to any woman, mother, sister, or lover."

The woman's intuitive deduction and subtle warning sent a blush burning across Kristine's cheeks. She'd been a fool to succumb to her longings and his desire. He'd had other lovers. She'd known that simple truth from his first kiss. He'd left them all, and less than an hour ago he had professed a need to leave her too. Lois hadn't brought the boy home, and she'd just told Kristine she doubted if the younger woman could hold the man.

"Was there something wrong with the data?"

Kristine asked, drawing the personal vein of the conversation to an abrupt close.

"The map." Lois opened the top folder and flipped through the pages until she found what she wanted. "It's missing an important piece of information."

Kristine had studied every iota of his research and had found nothing missing. In truth, it was the most complete report she'd ever seen. "What's missing?" She looked and still didn't know.

"The location of Chatren-Ma."

Kristine gave Lois a quizzical glance. Maybe the woman wasn't as sharp as she'd believed. No, she quickly amended. Lois Shepherd was plenty smart. Maybe the trip had tired her out.

"He's put the maps together in a series of enlargements," she explained in a brisk tone, keeping her doubt to herself so as not to embarrass the woman. "The first map, here, where he's lifted out a section, refers to the second map where the section is enlarged. The series continues through all five maps until he gets down to the illustrations and photographs of the monastery." Kristine didn't know how anyone could have done a more thorough job.

Lois did, though. "He lost some latitude and longitude on the way, and he doesn't pick it back up."

"Well, yes," Kristine agreed. It was true. He hadn't marked degrees on every single map, but with a little figuring and backtracking, a person could pinpoint a fly on one of the stone walls.

Or could they? She flipped forward a few pages, holding the bearings in her head until she reached the map where they stopped. Okay, she thought, returning to the previous page, now all a person had to do was . . . wonder what Kit was up to.

She checked again, comparing the two maps. The consecutive enlargement was out of kilter, off just enough to make it useless.

Lois tapped a lot of numbers into her calculator and said dryly, "I don't think he wants anyone within a fifty-mile radius of the place, or . . . Just a second. Make that a fifty-two-point three-mile radius." She looked up, her eyes wide. "That's a helluva lot of country up there to go wandering around in."

"It's an oversight," Kristine said, staunchly defending him.

Lois didn't buy it. "Kit Carson has never made an unintentional oversight in his life. The boy is holding out on me."

And me, Kristine silently added, shifting her gaze to his broad back. What in the hell *was* he up to? With time she would have discovered the deception herself, after he'd gone, when her anger wouldn't have had such a handy target. He'd promised her his knowledge of Chatren-Ma, and he'd delivered everything except the damn location. What kind of bimbo did he think she was?

The kind of bimbo who fell in love and in bed with a barbarian she barely knew, she answered herself. The kind of sex-starved female who responded to the first man with enough charm and enough skill to make her feel what she had thought could never be hers.

She wasn't going to die, and she wasn't going to disappear. The spell was beginning to crack a little, and if she still knew she would spend weeks and months of days and nights missing him after he'd gone, she wasn't admitting to the weakness. Not yet.

"Where is it, Kit?" She spoke loud enough to capture both men's attention.

"Direct and to the point," Lois murmured beside her. "I like that."

"Where's what?" Thomas asked.

Kit didn't need further explanation. He saw the maps spread on the table. "I think the ladies have discovered a slight discrepancy. Lo-eese, I believe, understands. Kreestine less so."

"You can't hide it forever, Kit," Lois said, usurping Kristine's next broadside with a volley of her own. "Word is already out that you made a major find, and when those blocks go on exhibition, everyone is going to know exactly where you've been."

"Without knowing exactly where I've been," he added, emphasizing his own point.

Kristine kept her silence, letting Lois fight the battle. The older woman was much better prepared to win, and Kristine suddenly knew she had no place in the famous trio. Kit had granted her entrée onto the playing field, but from the moment he'd said he wanted to go home, she'd felt more and more like the outsider she was. Kit's "oversight" had only made it perfectly clear.

She didn't know how she could be worthy of his love and remain unworthy of his trust, unless what they'd shared hadn't been love. Maybe out of her own need she'd imagined his deeper responses. She wasn't an expert. What did she know of the difference between sex and love. People more worldly than she had been confusing the two for centuries. Or was it just women who got confused, while men got what they wanted? For sure as she sat there, she was getting more confused by the minute.

"You may or may not be the best, Kit," Lois said after a tense pause, "but you're not the only one with enough mental and financial resources to track down the Chatren-Ma. If we know where it is, we can organize some protection, let the world know there is something worth protecting."

Kit laughed, but it was a cynical sound. It unnerved Kristine more than his leaving, more than his subterfuge, making her doubt everything she felt for him. "The world has shown little interest in protecting that which I hold dear. You know this, Lo-eese."

"Somebody is going to find it, Kit. Don't you think it would be wise to inform the Chinese before the Turk—"

"He will never find it," Kit interrupted her harshly.

"He's got the backing."

"Money will not buy entrance into Chatren-Ma, nor craft or cunning. That one's beliefs will forever bar the door."

For the first time, a ripple appeared in Lois's professional demeanor. "Don't go mystical on me, Kit. I'm talking facts."

"And I speak the truth. There *is* a difference."

Lois stared at him for a long moment, like a mother looking at a recalcitrant child she couldn't control. Then she began shoving folders, papers, maps, folios, and everything else into her briefcase. "When you reconcile the two, give me a call. I'm the one footing the bill. Thomas, let's get this stuff into that rented tuna boat you call a Cadillac."

Kristine saw them out after all the boxes were loaded, but she didn't wait around to see who won the argument on how to conserve archaeological sites. She was angry and trying not to be hurt. People fell in and out of bed all over the place, she knew. She also knew, if given the chance, she'd fall in bed with him all over again. She had to be nuts.

She needed to think everything through, find a bit of contemporary panache to put sex in the right perspective. She would still have her published credit, but the university had promised her that, not Kit. She'd still have a ton of information on the *Kāh-gyur* itself, but that wasn't what he'd promised her. He'd pledged a legend, Chatren-Ma, and that was what she wanted. She wasn't a scientist; she was a historian. She dealt in spans of time and spreads of men and culture. She needed the authentication of the artifacts to confirm the ideas behind them. She needed the location of Chatren-Ma to prove it existed.

And damn it all, she needed him. No amount of panache could change what she felt. No amount of confusion could smother the hurt.

Nine

She'd talk to him, Kristine decided. That was what she'd do. She'd talk to him and explain how she felt.

No, she wouldn't. Only a fool would expose herself.

She threw another handful of party trash into her garbage bag and bent down to pick a napkin up off the floor. If he loved her, if he was everything he'd led her to believe, he wouldn't have disappeared into the garage after Shepard and Stein had left. He would have read her mind and come back inside, come back to her with reassurances on his lips and comfort in his touch.

She'd be cool. That's what she'd be. Cool, calm, and collected. Mature. Sophisticated.

She knelt down to retrieve a cashew from under the coffee table. She'd be so cool, he'd need a polar jacket to keep his blood above freezing.

No, she wouldn't. Too much cool was overkill, a

dead giveaway, even supposing she could pull it off. She'd be reasonable, she told herself, scooting farther under the table after a cracker crumb. Reasonableness would drive him crazy.

No, it wouldn't. She sighed. Nothing could drive him crazy. The man had serenity down to a fine art, and she was a mass of doubts and conflicting emotions without an ounce of serenity in sight.

But he hadn't been serene when he made love with her. He'd been warm and wild, as hungry as she for the pleasure they'd created. Of course, making love with him again couldn't exactly be construed as a strategic move, not by anyone's standards, not even with her most convoluted logic.

Too bad. The regret whispered across her mind. She immediately squelched the wayward thought. Making love with him again, indeed. What did she think she was made of? Steel? How much did she think her heart could take? She already felt a little mangled around the edges.

He'd given her one thing, though. He'd proven John Garraty wrong. Lord, what a painful lesson it might turn out to be.

Out of the corner of her eye she caught sight of a flickering shadow crossing the deck, and she quickly backed out from under the table. The last place she wanted him to find her was crawling on the floor. She had to avoid such an abject display of her feelings for as long as she could hold out.

Anger was what she needed, unbridled anger, fiery with the cause of justice. He'd made a promise.

So where was it? she thought in disgust, waiting for even a spark of rage to light up her misery. There wasn't any rage to be found, only the heartache she felt in anticipation of his leaving. How in the world could she have done something as stupid as fall in love with him?

Ah, there it was, the first flame of fury, and in the nick of time. She heard the outside door to her office open, and fleetingly wondered why he hadn't used the front door or the back. Both were closer to the garage than the office door.

She studiously ignored his approach, busying herself with tidying up. If his tread sounded a mite heavier, and if his presence seemed a shade darker behind her, she discounted it for one moment before he grabbed her.

With the first touch of his hand she knew it wasn't Kit, but as that hand was firmly clapped over her mouth, and an iron-hard arm was squeezing the very breath out of her, she could do little more than struggle in silence and pray she didn't faint.

In the end Kit had compromised with Shepherd and Stein. He'd promised to give them the exact location before they exhibited the pieces, which bought him a year, maybe two, to get himself back into Nepal, a year to soothe ruffled, officious feathers, a year to find a way into Tibet and return to Chatren-Ma. One glimpse had not been nearly enough. More than the *Kāh-gyur* rested under those stones. He'd felt something ancient and powerful.

There would be no compromise with Kristine, though. He'd made a promise to her, and he planned on making many more, all the promises of a lifetime shared.

A soft smile curved his mouth. He'd waited throughout the rest of the day for the night to come, for the moon to rise and chase the sun from the sky. Then she would be his again.

He lifted the lid on the trunk by his bed and slipped his skinning knife into his palm. With care, he pried a thin block of wood from the side panel, and with equal care caught an edge of parchment with the blade and pulled the paper into the light. His first gift to her would fulfill his first promise, the only map known to man with the location of Chatren-Ma. Her distress over Lois's discovery had touched him from across the room. He'd underestimated the older woman's talents, or he would have taken the time to reassure Kristine beforehand.

He lowered the lid and spread the map over the top of the trunk, his hands smoothing out the folds—then fear, stark and chaotic and distinctly Kristine's, rushed in at him from all sides.

Too late. The truth hit him cold and hard even as he raced from the room. He grabbed his *khukri* from where it hung by the door and vaulted over the side railing, landing lightly on the ground and taking off again.

He passed the backdoor, loosing Mancos with a quick flick of his fingers. "Go!" he ordered.

But neither he nor the dog was fast enough. The house was empty, and so would Kit's heart have been if not for the rage boiling up from the very bottom of his soul. It seeped into his pores from a resting place he'd long denied, consuming him. It blinded him and yanked his muscles into tight, tight knots.

Careless! The word seared his conscience. He'd

grown soft, dangerously soft, in the luxury of her company.

Forcing his mind to blankness, he retraced his footsteps, swearing vengeance with every pace. He swore vengeance for her fear. He swore vengeance for the violation of her home, and if need be, he swore death for her life.

He found the office door ajar and rattled it off its hinges with a vicious kick. He whirled around and stormed out of the room, still searching.

In the living room, tossed among the clutter of napkins and glasses on the coffee table, he found what he had searched for. A bronze panther coiled flat on a three-inch disc, the Turk's calling card; and beneath the metal plaque, his own likeness sketched on a wanted poster from Xizang, formerly the country of Tibet.

The price beneath the face left no doubts in Kit's mind about the Turk's motivation or his destination. The Chinese wanted him more than they wanted the *Kāh-gyur*. Much more.

"This they shall have," he vowed in a low growl, pricking the poster with the tip of his blade. "And they shall pay dearly for the pleasure of my company."

With deadly, lightninglike grace, he turned on the balls of his feet, releasing the knife at the apex of his rising swing. The blade landed with a thudding twang, impaling the poster to a solid oak cupboard door.

The Turk would be moving fast, a stranger in an unwelcoming land. He'd avoid the embassies. The Chinese didn't want a hostage, they wanted Kautilya Carson. The Turk would run for home, but he'd find no refuge there. He'd find he had no place left to run.

Kit packed light, taking only his chamois bag. He stopped once more at the house, levering his knife out of the cupboard door and stuffing the wanted poster in his pocket. In the laundry room, he used the blade to slash open a fifty-pound bag of dog food.

"Pace yourself, Mancos," he suggested to the dog who followed him from room to room. "Kreestine will be back within two weeks. You know where the reservoir is. Straight down and straight back, no fooling around."

At the front door, he knelt down to unlatch the dog door, then turned and laid his hand on the dog's huge head, scratching him behind the ears. "Lay low during the day. Drink at night. Sleep in your own bed, and if you eat the furniture, there'll be hell to pay. Understand?"

The dog whined, his jowls quivering.

"Don't worry, Mancos. I'll send her home. One way or the other, I'll get her back where she belongs." He slowly rose and sheathed his knife. *And if the Turk denies me this, I'll know it on his last breath. You have my promise.*

Let's see, Kristine thought, fighting through a veil of disorientation. First you were in the living room, then slung over a shoulder, then nothing, then a little airplane noise, then another bigger nothing, then a whole lot of airplane noise.

And now this place. If she hadn't been scared senseless, the smell definitely would have offended her. The dark, windowless room reeked of old fish, lots of old, dead, decaying fish. The concrete floor was wet and slimy with stuff she didn't want to identify. She was almost glad it was too dark to see.

Voices from outside pierced the veil more clearly than her own feeble thoughts. She concentrated on them, but after a minute or two wished she hadn't. She could read and write Chinese, a spattering of Tibetan, a little less Nepali, and understood very little of the spoken word in any of them.

But the voices told her she was somewhere in Asia, somewhere on the coast if the smell were any clue, which effectively eliminated Tibet and Nepal.

Great. She'd always loved to travel, though she usually saw a few more of the sights.

Rising on shaky legs, she tried to take stock of her surroundings and her situation. The surroundings were simple—that smell. She approached her situation a little more thoroughly.

No one in their right mind would drag her halfway around the world just to kill her. Of course, she had no reason whatsoever to believe her abductors were in their right minds, but she'd accept the point out of necessity. It was either that or sink into panic.

They'd drugged her. Nothing else explained the blanks in her memory, and that fact pushed her closer to the panic she was trying to avoid. At home she was known to have a beer or two, or a glass of wine, but that was the extent of her substance abuse. Anything else smacked highly of idiocy in her book.

And this was all Kit Carson's fault, of that she had no doubts. He and his *Kāh-gyur* had gotten her into this fix. She didn't know exactly why.

Shepherd and Stein had taken the artifacts, and wasn't that what everyone had been after?

"Right," she whispered, and discovered she liked the sound of her own voice. So she whispered some more. "They want the *Kāh-gyur*, not me, and all that guy with the big shoulders has to do is ask, and I'll tell him everything I know. I'll get him an engraved invitation to the Natural History Museum of Los Angeles County, Los Angeles, California." She squeezed her eyes shut and forced her mind to think, finally coming up with a ZIP code she'd typed about a hundred times in the last few days.

"Nine, zero, zero, zero, seven. I'll call Lois personally and put him on the phone, let him deal with an expert instead of a nobody history professor from some obscure western university." She paused and mentally backtracked. "Okay, okay, a not-so-obscure western university, but no ivy leaguer either. Damn you, Kit." She edged along the wall, hoping to run into a door, an unlocked door, and maybe a car outside. A car with keys in the ignition and a map on the front seat.

"And a plane ticket in the glove compartment, a plane ticket anywhere, and food, something light, nongreasy." Her wish list grew and grew, until she had herself set up in a Ritz Carlton with a sunken tub, expensive soap, and room service where everyone spoke English, preferably American English.

A rattling sound off to her right abruptly burst her bubble. The door she'd been nowhere close to finding swung open on rusty hinges, flooding the fishhouse with painfully bright sunshine.

Cringing against the wall, she peaked through

the slits she made with her fingers, and a very unladylike expletive lodged in her throat.

The man who had broken into her house, the man she'd caught a glimpse of during one of her moments of consciousness, was more than shoulders. He was arms, huge arms, and long, muscular legs, and a barrel chest, and for the life of her she couldn't imagine why he'd attempted to take Kit's plait, for his own hung to his waist in a corded ebony swath.

"I am the Turk." He smiled, a slow, barbarous smile that lit a face of indeterminate origin, making Kristine wonder just how many cultural half-breeds were running around loose on the Tibetan Plateau. "And you are mine."

Perfect, she thought. *Absolutely, grade-A perfect. Damn you, Kit Carson. I'm not sure how long I've been gone, but if you're not at least halfway over the Pacific by now, somebody is going to be in a whole lot of trouble . . . probably me.*

Kit slid off the mare's back and let the reins fall to the ground. He'd traveled the width of the Pacific Ocean and almost half as far again in four days, putting himself deep inside the forbidden land and closer to the Turk's stronghold than he'd ever wanted to be again. His home lay over two hundred miles to the south, past the Tsangpo River and the wall of the Himalayas.

He hadn't come back to go home. He'd come for Kristine and the Turk's throat. He'd missed them in Shanghai, and had been slipping and sliding through the authorities' fingers since his first step on China's soil. Now he was beyond their reach in

Tibet, long gone in the shadow of the mountains where the land stretched for mile after mile of emptiness, touched but unchanged by man.

Light played across the terrain in ever deepening shades of twilight blue and rosy pink, turning to purple and black in the net of canyons spread out before him. The ground shifted in a colored patchwork of red iron, grays, and ocher, down to the tawny dust of the canyon floors.

He sat on the cliff edge, waiting, letting the light and darkness and color wash over him, blown by the ceaseless wind. Behind him his horse snorted and tossed her head, filling the night air with the music of harness bells. All else was quiet, from the mountains at his back to the northern horizon.

Seconds melted into minutes, minutes built into hours, and the the moon rose high in the sky. Still he waited and watched, ever patient, ever angry.

Before dawn, his wait ended. He slowly uncrossed his legs and rose to his knees, setting his metal cup of tea aside. Far below on the canyon floor, lantern lights twinkled and disappeared with the irregularity of the contours of the land. It was a caravan, moving to the west and the fortress that lay there, waiting for its master and for the prey to rise to the bait.

Kit whistled softly, and the mare carefully approached the drop-off, her hooves sending up feathery puffs of dust. He stood up and pulled his rifle from the saddle scabbard, loading a single cartridge into the chamber.

Lowering himself flat to the ground, he settled the stock against his shoulder and sighted down the barrel. A moment later the echo of his shot ricocheted along the canyon walls, and one of the lanterns extinguished in a quick burst of flame. The other lights quickly followed into darkness, snuffed by the riders who held them.

The Turk had been warned; he knew someone was after him. When he reached home he would know who, and after that there would be no more warnings.

Kit rose to his feet, sheathed the rifle, and returned his metal cup to the saddlebag. Then he swung himself onto the mare's back and turned her toward the mountains and Chatren-Ma.

Barbarian, Kristine had quickly learned, was a relative term. Any historian or archaeologist who shared a meal with the Turk would be hard-pressed to apply the term to Kit Carson.

The man ate with his hands, and his fingers, and his teeth, in a manner she found just short of dealing death to her own appetite. But what his table manners didn't accomplish, his dark-eyed gaze did. He followed her every move, no matter how slight, with an intensity she was sure exposed her deepest thoughts.

He was welcome to most of them, since they expressed a loathing she didn't have the courage to voice aloud. There were a few she'd rather keep to herself, however. The ones dreading the lust-ful curiosity she saw in the midnight depths of his eyes, the one verging on panic whenever he reached out with a bronzed hand to trace a path across her skin. If Kit was masculinity at its gentlest and most invincible, the Turk was mas-culinity in its most arrogant and brutish form, handsome in a way no single-race man would ever be.

Two days ago, when he'd taken her from that foul fishhouse in Shanghai, his arrogance had been nearly palpable. He'd all but sneered as he toyed with her hair, then tossed her a brightly colored wool skirt, cotton shirt, a black vest, and low leather boots, and told her to get dressed. They were leaving in five minutes.

She didn't get much else out of him as they traveled by small plane across the breadth of China to Tibet. She did manage to ask him how he'd smuggled her out of the United States. She would have thought a drugged and unconscious woman, even one as slight as she, couldn't be that easy to hide. He'd only laughed, made some comment about greedy Americans, then told her he'd done no more than bribe some antiquity dealers in Los Angeles with various religious objects and a tapestry stolen from Buddhist shrines and temples, and they had arranged for a plane to fly him and his "cargo" to Shanghai, with no customs officials bothering to check that cargo.

The Turk's arrogance was gone now, however. Now he was nervous, hair-triggered to every breath taken by anyone in his presence. The shot at dawn had turned his cocksure demeanor to wariness. What he'd found half an hour later embedded in the gate to his compound—a *khukri* sunk to the hilt, spearing the torn halves of a wanted poster, a quarter section of map, and a yard's length of roan braid—had twisted his wariness into fear. No mere man had accomplished the feat of sinking twelve inches of blade through solid wood.

"Kautilya wants you back." The Turk's silken

voice startled her into looking up, something she'd been avoiding. "More so than I had thought possible."

Kristine kept her silence, watching him with her own mixture of wariness and fear. Kit was out there, somewhere in the night. All she had to do was keep herself together until he came.

The Turk leaned forward and dropped another stick of wood on the fire burning in a pit in the middle of the kitchen's dirt floor. They were alone in the room. Guards had been posted in the compound, and the other bandits had retired to bedrooms on the second floor, or to one of the other houses chinked together against the canyon wall.

Goats, pigs, and chickens milled about the stone-walled courtyard fronting the main house, adding a strangely domestic ambience to the hideaway. The two blacker-than-sin mastiffs chained to the door, however, kept her from being lulled into anything but the barest surface calm.

Stacks of woolen bags filled with salt and grains were piled high against three of the kitchen's inner walls, giving the room the look of the inside of a quilted tent. Piled on the other side of the room were several crates of rifles, which Kristine bet were "trade goods." Nobody needed that much firepower for personal reasons.

"I expected him to come, yes, but out of a sense of duty," the Turk continued. "He has a great sense of duty, Kautilya does. But this . . ." He lifted the roan braid and let it slide through his fingers back to the table. "This is more than duty." A frown etched deep lines into his lean cheeks. "I cannot help but wonder what you are to him, Kreestine Richards."

She watched him stretch lazily back in his chair, then felt his booted foot slide next to hers.

"Maybe you are worth more to him than he is to the Chinese?" A wolfish smile replaced the frown, showing a flash of crooked, brown teeth.

She jerked her foot back under her chair. If Kit had ever smiled at her with that much feral intent, she would have sent him packing long before he'd had a chance to steal to her heart like the outlaw he truly had become.

She'd seen the poster and thought the sum the Chinese offered was just short of unbelievable, but she had no sympathy and no answer to the Turk's dilemma. She didn't know where the greatest profit lay. She couldn't place a price on her life, let alone guess Kit's price on her life. But he'd already given the Turk more than he'd given her, a fourth of the map to Chatren-Ma.

All in all, she was having a hell of a time sorting everything out. If he gave the Turk what he'd promised her in order to save her life, did that mean he'd broken his word? At this point, she really didn't give a darn about Chatren-Ma, but the complicated ethics of the problem were a preferable focus for her mind than the gleam in the Turk's eye.

"He has had many women," the Turk said. "But the only time he ever risked his life for one was the night he took mine, the night I took this." He fingered the braid again.

Oh brother, she didn't want to hear this. She really didn't.

"That he was unaware of the female's pledge to me meant little to me then, but I wonder, Kreestine, are you pledged to him?"

She wasn't going to touch that one with a ten-foot pole. All she wanted to do was go home. What was Kit waiting for? Why hadn't he rescued her? He'd had the whole day to think of something.

Good Lord! What was *she* thinking? The unprecedented selfishness of her thoughts hit home with a disturbing force.

Slumping over the table, she dropped her head into her hands. It was Kit's life she was bartering away. His life she was willing to risk for only a chance at her own freedom. She couldn't do it. She couldn't give the Turk another weapon.

"No," she murmured, shaking her head, finally breaking the silence she'd used for sanctuary. Even as she spoke, she prayed her words weren't true. "I am not pledged to Kautilya Carson. I am nothing to him. Nothing."

The Turk's low chuckle filled the room, then he pushed his chair back.

"You lie, Kreestine, but such a sweet lie." He rounded the table and encircled her wrists with one large, rough hand, pulling her to her feet, close to his chest. She turned her head aside, hiding her face against her shoulder, but the strength of his fingers grasping her chin forced her to meet his gaze.

"Sang Phala, it seems, chose no more of a monk to replace me than the one I would have been." His deep voice, so near, so soft, caressed her fears to new life; and the rock-solid body pressed against hers put the raw edge of terror on those fears. Neither, though, had the impact of his words.

"You!" she gasped. The Turk was Sang Phala's nephew, whom Sang Phala had traded . . . to bandits . . . for Kit. Any flicker of hope Kristine might have nurtured, died.

"For too long I have been second to Kautiiya. I will not take his leavings tonight." He released her, and the breath rushed back into her lungs. "But if on the morrow he loses . . ." His voice trailed off in an unspoken threat.

Loses what? Kristine wondered, steadying herself with a hand on the table. Surely not his life. She'd read the characters on the poster. The Chinese wanted the outlaw Carson alive.

And what of her? What would become of her if Kit couldn't save her? Would she be forever trapped in this lost land, some barbarian bandit's moll?

The worst of her thoughts didn't bear thinking, but neither would they be put to rest. They loomed large and impregnable in her mind, like the broad back the Turk turned to her as he lay down on his pallet.

The fire drew her gaze to its glowing embers, and in every flash of energy, every shift of flame, she saw spice-colored eyes, gentle and mysterious, beckoning her to sleep . . . and to dream of him.

Ten

They rode at dawn. Or rather the bandits rode and Kristine held on for dear life, her fingers tangled in a whipping ebony mane. Not that she needed to hold on, for the Turk held her securely in his iron grip on the horse's blanketed back. Powerful muscles bunched and stretched beneath her as the steed's flying hooves pounded the ground. But they were no more powerful than the arm wrapped around her waist or the long thighs flanking hers.

Icy wind bit at her cheeks, contrasting sharply with the heat of the masculine body surrounding her from behind. He'd given her a full-length sheepskin coat to wear, the leather softly tanned and embroidered with bright threads of gold and blue, red and green, and the downy fleece turned inward to warm her and caress her skin.

The quarter map Kit had impaled on the compound gate led them out of the canyons to a rocky plain, and then into the next set of canyons beyond. The sun had not yet penetrated the chasms stretched out before them, and after hours of riding at a mile-eating pace, the band slowed their wild mounts, picking their way through the labyrinth of towering walls.

The Turk repeatedly checked the map, leading his men deeper into the maze of rock. More than one bandit cast a wary glance behind himself as the canyons twisted and turned upon one another. A half an hour in, water began gathering in small pools on the ground, running down the striated earth and adding a melodic backdrop to the splashing hooves. Soon the pools connected into a gently flowing stream and mists began to rise, slowly at first, barely a wisp of lightness here and there on the canyon floor. But the farther they went, the thicker the mist became, obscuring both the sight and the sound of the horse's legs.

Sitting on the lead pony and in front of the Turk, Kristine felt as if she were pushing a vanguard through the fog. The low white cloud drifted down the canyon ahead of them, rolling and billowing, rising ever higher. It hung like gossamer whiffs of smoke released from the black stone that pressed in on them from either side. Unconsciously, she scooted closer to the Turk. His arm tightened around her, as if he, too, needed some kind of reassurance in this strange place Kautilya had brought them to.

A muted whinny from far behind them caused them both to jerk their heads around. Kristine couldn't control her gasp of dismay, nor the Turk his grunt of surprise. They were surrounded, enveloped by the mists that not only rose before them, but closed behind them as well.

Three other riders, as wild eyed as the horses they rode, floated in and out of the swirling white mass, only three of the ten who'd left with them at dawn.

The Turk jerked hard on the reins, wheeling his horse about, but the animal moved no farther, stopped in midwhirl by a soft whistle penetrating the stillness.

Kristine's heart lodged in her throat, beating furiously. Kit!

But where?

She scanned the emptiness around her, trying to see past the fog, but to no avail. The world was invisible. She turned to the Turk, but the barely masked fear chiseled on his face forced her gaze back to the riders. One by one, in growing stupefaction, she watched them being swallowed up by mists.

"You fool!" she said fiercely, turning on the man who held her and cuffing him on the shoulder. His eyes quickly lost their glazed expression, flashing at her with the same combination of fear and anger she felt inside herself. "Don't you know any better than to—"

"Quiet, woman!" he ordered.

"—let your enemy make your choices for you?" she finished anyway, compelled by her quickening panic. She didn't know who to trust anymore. Kit had gotten her into this, and she'd be damned if she liked his methods of getting her out.

The stallion shifted restlessly beneath them, transferring his unease to the people astride his back. Kristine tightened her grip on the mane. By God, if she was going to disappear, she wasn't going to do it without the horse.

The soft whistle cut through the air again, and the horse picked up first one hoof, then another, following a path only he could see. A rifle came into view at Kristine's side, brushing her arm.

"I *think* it's a little late for that, *bucko*," she gritted through her teeth. She wasn't worried for Kit. He obviously had everything under control. Everything. From the horse, to her, the Turk, and the very elements of the air.

But how much control could one man wield when he turned it on nature and this maze of earth and troubled sky?

Things of power . . . The phrase came back to her, haunting in its accuracy. She'd fallen in love with a man so far above her on the evolutionary scale, there could be no hope for it. If she'd had even an ounce of adrenaline to spare, she would have used it to salve her breaking heart. But survival had a funny way of superseding all other emotions, and her survival was very much in doubt at the moment.

Could he even see her, feel her presence, in this quagmire? She hadn't made much of a mark in the outside world, where everything was more cut and dried, more crystal clear. How could she possibly be making an impact on the bottom of a canyon to nowhere?

The stallion suddenly picked up his pace, snorting and tossing his head. Kristine bounced along for a few yards, until he broke into a full-stride gallop.

"Damn him," she heard the Turk curse as he leaned low over her back, flattening her against the horse's neck.

The hell-bent ride through the shifting white

blindness seemed an unfitting end for a woman who had lived her life in relative calm, until an auburn-haired stranger had shown up on her doorstep. Her life had taken a turn for the worse that day—and a definite but terribly short-lived turn for the better, she admitted in the one small part of her mind not consumed with her last prayers.

The canyon walls moved ever closer, the stream grew ever deeper, and still the stallion plunged on, driven by forces Kristine was incapable of understanding and the Turk couldn't control.

Suddenly the canyon ended in a blank wall of stone. Kristine instinctively braced herself for the inevitable crash, but the Turk hauled back on the reins, crushing her within the straining vise of his arms. The horse reared and screamed, and the echoes of that shrill cry reverberated down the length of their tomb.

Before the stallion could recover his footing, the Turk swung his leg over the hindquarters, dragging her with him off the raging beast.

So help her God, Kristine thought, slumping over the Turk's arm, if the Turk didn't get to him first, she just might murder Kit herself.

As a rescue attempt, his was failing on all counts. Scaring her to death was proving to be as effective and far more imaginative than anything the Turk might have come up with. She didn't have a breath left in her body, or a muscle in working order.

"Will you die for her, Turk?"

The voice came from above them, disembodied by the mists, ringing with cold sincerity, and followed by the authority of a neatly placed gunshot. The Turk flinched and almost dropped her.

One-handed, he swung his rifle up and fired a return shot.

"And I ask once more. Will you die for her, Turk?" The voice came from a different direction.

The Turk jerked her around and fired again. Kristine knew if she'd had even half her normal strength, she could break away from him. And truly, being between two men shooting at each other seemed the most dangerous position of the three. All the nothingness around her, though, kept her firmly by the Turk's side, or rather, firmly in front of him. She'd rather die where she stood than get swallowed up.

Ah, Kreestine . . . where is your faith?

"Oh, no," she whispered shakily. "Oh, no, you don't."

"Silence!" the Turk hissed, tightening his arm around her. Kristine tightened right back, grabbing him wherever she could get a handhold.

And your courage, my love?

"Hah!" she scoffed. "Try about ten thousand miles back!"

"Silence, I say!"

He got it, about a ton and a half of it in deafening stillness. The eeriness of so much silence gnawed at her nerves and his. Even the stallion had disappeared.

Kit grinned down at them from where he knelt on his lofty perch, well satisfied with the state of her mind and the courage she denied. He took a moment—and only a moment—to rest his forehead on his upraised knee, thanking the gods for sending her to him. The meteorologically induced mists of Chatren-Ma would lift with the noonday sun, when shafts of light struck the canyon floor and warmed the air. He wanted her back before then.

The bandit was a Bonpo, a believer in shamans and demons. Kit had lured him to a place where both might reside, resisting the fierce urge for immediate reprisal in the Turk's compound, where death would have been the only answer. Kit knew the exact limit of his own skills, and he knew the Turk's. The match was too close to call with a degree of safety for Kristine.

But in Chatren-Ma he held the deciding factor— fear. The Turk couldn't avoid it, and Kit had faced it before, in this very place. He'd gotten lost in the early morning mists on his search for the *Kāh-gyur*. They'd sneaked up on him, lapping at his feet, then his ankles, and all too quickly his knees.

The Turk was feeling their power now. Kit sensed his fear, and Kristine's. For that he had regrets.

To further his goal he took aim again.

The Turk jumped, swore, and thrust Kristine away from him, but not before she saw the seam on the sleeve his coat slice open. It was the last thing she saw, for in her next breath she was swallowed up.

Shadows moved within shadows, surrounding her with damp fingers of trailing moisture.

"Kit?" she whispered. When no answer was forth-coming, she tried another name, a name filled with as much mystery as the place. "Kautilya?"

Still nothing.

She took a tentative step with her hand out-stretched, searching for the canyon wall. She found more nothing. Had he moved the earth too?

Kit dropped off the ledge, landing on his feet

with his knees bent, and fired another shot. It would be so easy to kill the Turk, but the compassion he'd forsworn five days before stayed his hand. Sang Phala had not left him, and the old man had not trained him for murder.

Yet he would have a token for this week's work, and he would retrieve his *khukri*. He checked Kristine and fired again at the Turk, urging the man farther away, down toward a cut in the wall, taking more cloth from the left side of his thick wool coat so the Turk would not mistake his direction.

Kristine kept creeping away from the sound of gunfire, one inching step at a time, drawn by what she thought was a lifting of the mists ahead of her. Soon she could see her hand in front of her face. Then the stone of the canyon wall came into view.

And then Chatren-Ma.

Kit knelt on the ground, swearing softly to himself. He should have known better than to leave her on her own. She'd physically wandered off the way her mind often wandered off, on a tangent he hadn't foreseen. But what set his teeth on edge and tightened his hand into a fist were things she hadn't foreseen.

Chatren-Ma was not a place for doubts or the faint of heart, or for a believer in anything but truth. He loved her, yes, but only she knew the strength of her own base mettle. If she hadn't found it yet, she soon would. He needed to be there in case what she found was not enough.

He traced the imprint of her foot in the dust, then slowly lifted his gaze to the towering shelf of rock rimmed with a black slash. She'd passed through the shadow. He had no choice but to follow where he'd planned on going alone.

Difficult but not impossible, Kristine thought, eyeing the narrow gap on the trail. She would have gone back hours ago if the opportunity had arisen, but she'd gotten herself good and lost, and high. Oh brother, had she gotten herself high.

The ledge she stood on dropped away in a dizzying fall of thousands of feet. Vertigo, though, wasn't her problem. The gap was a definite problem. Maybe more of a problem than she could handle, and she still wasn't any closer to the monastery carved into the canyon wall. There had to be a trick to it.

"More than one, Kreestine," Kit said from above her.

He startled her, but she had the good sense not to jump, or even to twitch too much.

"Hi." Her voice sounded hushed and insignificant against the radiant panorama spread out before her in mile after endless mile of sun-baked, gilt-edged landscape. The rift valley pushed the canyon walls even farther apart, leaving room for a river basin to widen and flow over the acres of stone tumbled from the cliffs.

She didn't bother to wonder where he'd come from. She'd been lost in the maze of paths scoring the cliff-face long enough to know they had more secrets than the CIA. She'd popped out of nowhere a couple of times herself, to find herself dangling over a whole lot of nothing.

"Give me your hand," he said, "and I'll pull you up."

A sensible request, but she wasn't buying.

"What happened to the bandits in the mist?" she asked, not daring to look up, which she'd discovered was much worse than looking down.

"They are probably home by now."

"And the Turk?"

"That one has a long walk, but he is young and strong, and maybe his horse will stop for him." He paused, then added, "Maybe not. The stallion was running pretty fast when I released him. He found my mare less accommodating than he'd wished."

"Oh," she said, finally understanding what had turned the not exactly docile animal into a nostril-flaring, head-tossing beast. "You planned for everything, didn't you."

"Almost." She heard his heavy sigh. "Give me your hand, please, Kreestine."

She still had a hundred or so questions, and this time she was getting answers. "What about the mist? Did you do that?"

"You overestimate my talents. It is nothing more than that which happens every morning during this season. Nothing more than cold air condensing water vapor. The canyon is empty now."

"I've seen river mist," she said, her tone skeptical, "and that ain't it."

"We are in Chatren-Ma. There could be more, but not by my hand, and nothing I can explain."

She didn't know whether to feel better or not, or safer or not. She did know she couldn't stand on the ledge indefinitely. Her path had dead-ended . . . and Chatren-Ma still beckoned like a promise just beyond her grasp.

She had another question, something along the lines of "Why didn't you come for me yesterday?" or "What made you so sure the Turk wouldn't hurt me?" or even "Didn't you care that he had me at his mercy?" But no matter how she phrased it in her mind the words seemed too personal, the doubts too real to expose to a man she might have only slept with. A man who'd said he'd wanted to leave her, and then by some quirk of fate had found she'd left him first and shown up at the exact place he'd professed to want to go. Complicated stuff to be dealing with on a ledge barely wider than her foot was long.

She knelt and dusted her hands with dirt for traction. She had a job to do. She had a discovery and a name to make. Kristine Richards was on the road to glory, a damned tiny but guaranteed road to glory. Whereas love, it seemed, held no guarantees at all.

Turning to the stone wall behind her, she flattened herself against it and raised her arm high in the air. Strong, warm fingers wrapped around her wrist. She gripped his forearm with her other hand, and prayed he could lift a hundred and twenty-five pounds of dead weight. She helped where she could, jamming the toes of her boots into every nook and cranny the cliff offered, and trying to think light, trying to be light.

I'm a cloud, a mere tuft of cotton floating on the wind, lighter than the air, less substance than a dream.

She heard his labored breath, then his other hand clenched the collar of her coat. With a heave and a groan, he got most of her onto the upper path, she hung there, resting, her legs suspended in space.

He drew a deep breath and pulled again, and Kristine swung her knee onto the ledge. He pulled once more, rolling her on top of him as he collapsed on his back.

"You are no cloud, Kreestine," he said, gasping, "but it was a good thought."

They lay there for long moments, catching their breaths, and that more than anything proved to her he was a mortal man.

"Next time . . ." she said breathlessly. "Next time I'll send the coat up first."

"Good."

Still neither of them moved. She rested her head on his chest, checking out her new perch. His was a far cry better than the one she'd left. His was ten feet wide and had a good solid path carved in either direction. She could set up housekeeping on such a good ledge.

She turned her head in the other direction, toward the monastery, and felt his hand slide down her back in a gesture of comfort.

"Can we get there from here?" she asked, unaware of the wistfulness in her voice.

His smile teased her. "Only if you get off me. But truly the choice is yours, *bahini*. I have no complaints."

Chivalrous to the end, she thought, knowing what she looked like. He must have noticed, too, because he'd called her *bahini*. She'd looked the word up, and little sister was a far cry from wife, a

damn far cry from what they'd shared in her
bedroom. With a soft exhalation of air, she rolled
off him. She would have gotten up, except he
rolled, too, pinning her to the ground.

"You are well, then?" he asked.

"Pretty well," she hedged. Physically she was
fine, rather invigorated by the high mountain air
in fact. Any anger and anxiety she'd felt during her
ordeal had been subjugated by the sheer beauty
and the uncommon opportunities of the place
she'd been brought to. Emotionally, though, she'd
had a couple of major glitches, the cause of which
was looking down at her with such tender concern, she wondered if she was blowing them out of
proportion.

"You've been too long in the sun." His fingers
traced the bridge of her nose and caressed her
cheek.

"I forgot to pack my sunscreen," she said softly,
feeling the spell of him bind her anew and wishing
it wasn't so.

"Are you hungry?"

"Maybe." Her gaze fastened on the mouth mere
inches from her own, and she watched a smile
form.   .

"We have work to do, Kreestine, and quickly. I do
not wish to attempt the paths at night."

"Work?" she questioned, then silently cursed
herself. Of course, work. Wasn't that what she'd
just been telling herself?

His smile widened into a grin. "We are in Chatren-
Ma, *bahini*. I do not wish to leave empty-handed,
but I also know we should leave before dark."

An outlaw, his words confirmed in her mind. No
monk or mystic, but an outlaw to the core.

"You may come with me," he said. "I will not insist that you wait, but it would be my choice. I—" He stopped and reconsidered his words, then only said, "It would be my choice for you to wait."

"Not a chance," she said, looking him straight in the eye.

Eleven

"You have surprised me," Kit said, edging around a curve in the much narrowed trail and reaching a hand back to help her. "I did not think you would get this far on your own."

What could she say? Kristine mused. She was more than a little surprised herself.

"How did you get past the first avalanche?" he asked.

"Well, it wasn't exactly an avalanche." She grasped his hand and swung around the corner, coming up hard against the new cliff-face and letting out her breath. "I thought so at first, but then I noticed the boulders had a kind of pattern to them, like some-body had placed them there to block the trail, or a least give the appearance of having blocked the trail, and I figured anybody that determined to make an illusion had done it because the trail wasn't really blocked at all. It probably took me another fifteen minutes, though, to find the opening. I'd like to be able to date it, maybe shake up some conceptions on the early technological advances of a people still considered backward. It's a remarkable feat of engineering."

"Yes, a remarkable feat," Kit said, surprised again. It had taken him over an hour to find the opening the first time. "And Heaven's Steps?"

"Harder coming down than going up," she said with a nonchalance he would have been hard pressed to emulate. "What makes you think they were called Heaven's Steps?"

"There's an inscription carved into the stone at a juncture in the trail about twenty yards earlier." He edged around another crumbling precipice. "The words don't translate into English with precision, but they're very celestial."

"I don't remember a juncture twenty yards before the staircase." Talking helped, she thought, unwilling to look either up or down. Knowing the strength of his arm also helped.

His hand tightened on hers, and she glanced over at him. "You took the tunnel?" he asked.

She nodded. "I figured it would be kind of hard to fall off a tunnel."

She amazed him. She had more courage than he had thought, much more. He'd avoided the tunnel his first time in, but by the time he'd returned, he'd been forced into many tunnels, all of them to his detriment. There was no other way to enter Chatren-Ma. The monastery was impregnable from the valley floor. The sole access was from inside the earth, deep behind the cliff-face.

"Kreestine." He spoke her name with a note of gentle pride and a share of warning. "There are more tunnels ahead of us, and in many of them it would be an easy thing to fall off. The caverns are riddled with traps of emptiness for the unwary."

Traps of emptiness for the unwary, she slowly repeated in her mind, then caught his gaze. "You mean holes?"

"Holes," he confirmed, keeping his other knowledge to himself, not knowing how of if she'd be affected. "Big holes."

He was right, Kristine thought, edging around another "trap of emptiness." Without him guiding her, she would have disappeared about a mile back. She wasn't afraid of the dark, but she'd quickly worked up a steady stream of gratitude for Kit's presence. She was following him. She didn't know what he was following, but he hadn't missed yet.

"If you knew about the tunnels, why didn't you bring a flashlight?" she asked. If she'd known what she was getting into, she would have asked the Turk to stop someplace where she could have grabbed one of those halogen quartz things, or maybe two or three.

"Your eyes can deceive where your intuition will not fail. I spent many years, Kreestine, many years learning to see through the darkness of thoughts, learning to tread a path of light."

Lois wouldn't have liked his explanation, she mused. It was a little too mystical for the curator's pragmatic tastes. Kristine had no choice but to believe, and the only things she didn't like were the strained quality of his voice and the increasing heat of his hand in hers. She had a ridiculous urge to press the inside of her wrist against his forehead to see if he had caught a flu.

"You wouldn't have accidentally shot me, then?" she asked.

"You were safe from the minute the Turk discovered my knife in his door. The message was clear. He knew his life depended upon your safety. And—and the man I questioned in Shanghai assured me you were unhurt when he last saw you."

The hesitation in his voice and something about the way he said the word "questioned" bothered her. "Did you hurt him?" she asked quietly.

"I touched him, nothing more."

Touched him like he'd touched old Luke in the bar, she knew. "How did you get your knife into the compound gate?"

He hesitated again, as if reaching for a breath, then said very softly, "With much anger, Kreestine, much anger."

It was practically a declaration of love, but she wasn't going to push her luck. She was going to let the words float around inside her for a while, let them soak in, sort out. She knew what kind of man he was, and she was sure nothing short of the truest emotion, of undeniable need, could have snapped the rationality of his mind. The amount of anger he'd demonstrated left no room for rational anything. It must be love. But she wasn't going to push her luck.

"Come up behind me and put your arms around my waist," he said, his voice tense with concentration.

She did as she was told, keeping an inch of distance between them to help her ignore how good he felt, just in case she was wrong.

"Closer," Kit insisted, pulling her arms farther around him. "Match every step I take. Start . . . start with your right foot."

He was fighting a losing battle, and he cursed himself for a fool with every passing second weakening him. Because he'd had to hurry after her, he hadn't had the time to meditate, as he had before, focusing his energy so that all that was unseen in these tunnels could not distract him from the path. They couldn't turn back though. A thousand lost, soft-shod footsteps filled the caverns behind them, echoing through the centuries. They were dreams, thoughts with substance, and he heard every one, every question, every answer, trying to confuse him and make him lose the way. There was no evil, but there was warning, and certain death for an unsure footfall.

Kristine was another difference between the first time and this. Her strong will shone like a beacon behind him, attracting the ancient amalgamation of souls and the prayers they'd chanted into the rock. His sensitivity was both a blessing and a curse. He wasn't blind in the darkness. On the contrary, he saw too much, and he didn't know for how long he could handle it all.

They moved along a path Kristine could only guess at, one slow step at a time, for what seemed hours. She knew merely minutes had passed, but darkeness changed time, elongated it or suspended it altogether until a mark was met. It added an other-worldliness to the earth beneath her, to the walls around her. She couldn't see anything, but she felt . . . something.

In front of her, Kit stopped twice, three times, then four, and cursed softly at the fifth halt.

"Don't move." His voice echoed plainly, chasing the air into the dark void. *Don't move . . . don't move . . . don't . . . move . . .*

She felt one of his hands leave hers and shove

into his pocket. A striking sound came from the vicinity of his knife sheath, and a match flared. She took one look and froze like a rock.

She wanted to go home. She had no business being there, no history business, no love business, no sensible business. A gust of wind from somewhere extinguished the match.

He struck another, and Kristine looked again. She still wanted to go home.

They were balanced on a spit of land jutting out into a fathomless, floorless cavern, though land seemed too substantial a term for the bit of earth and stone beneath their feet. As if to confirm her opinion, an almost infinitesimal portion of pebble and dirt gave way, whispering off into the darkness. The match followed the fall, snuffing out in the abyss.

"We are almost there," Kit said. She forced herself to concentrate on his spoken words and not on the echoes wafting around them. "Let go of me, but do not move until you feel my hand around your ankle."

"Where are you going?" she whispered, trying to keep her own echoes out of the air.

"Over the edge."

"The edge?" Oh, she didn't like the sound of that, but he slipped away from her before she could voice an opinion or offer an alternative. Worse, she thought she heard him stumble, a man who could run on four-inch wide rails, a man whose grace exceeded that of the stars in the sky. She began to get very nervous.

Standing there on the small promontory, surrounded only by her own shallow breaths and a whole lot of timeless blackness, she discovered a few new things about herself. She was afraid of the dark after all; her balance, like his, didn't seem to be what it used to be—she swore she was swaying from side to side; and she'd picked a very interesting place to die.

She'd definitely make the news with this bit of folly.

"Krees, give me your hand."

This time she jumped at the opportunity, figuratively speaking.

He eased her over the edge, the front of her body sliding down the front of his. Suddenly the darkness filled with a crackling awareness. He pressed closer to her, closer than was absolutely necessary, she was sure.

She didn't mind the closeness, but she'd felt weakness in his arms where only strength had been before. He leaned against her, quietly, seriously.

"Are you okay?" she asked, smoothing loose strands of hair behind his ears and secretly checking his temperature. He was burning up.

"I missed you." His hand slowly rose to cup her face, and his voice grew husky. "I will not let anyone take you from me again."

He lowered his mouth and found what he searched for with her softly spoken, "Good."

The kiss was sweet, yet erotic in its creative intensity. His tongue slid across her lips, laving the tender skin before slipping inside the welcoming warmth of her mouth.

His groan echoed around her, heightening her senses and pushing her toward an edge she longed to fall off again, the one he'd taken her to when they'd made love.

Tonight, Kreestine, you will be mine. He deepened the kiss, the muscles in his arms tightening, giving her a taste of the power of his desire.

She sank under the pliant assault of his mouth, and she knew in her heart she could get addicted to his barbaric ways and Neanderthal tendencies. She would be his, indeed.

"We must go," he murmured weakly as he lifted his head, then he returned for another kiss, and yet another. "It is not far now."

The fathomless cavern actually proved to be about twenty fathoms deep, by her estimation of the rise between switchbacks. She doubted if she'd ever return, and certainly not without Kit, but even taking his phenomenal memory into account, she thought two heads full of catalogued facts were better than one. Especially since he seemed to be tiring at a rather accelerated pace.

The last tunnel grew narrower and narrower, giving Kristine her first bout with claustrophobia. The rough stone walls caught at her coat, the uneven floor twisted beneath her feet—rising up unexpectedly to trip her, then falling away in short, lurch-inducing drop-offs. She fell against him repeatedly. He caught her every time. And every time she felt his strength ebbing, and she started to know real fear of this strange place.

"What's happening to you, Kit?" she asked, trying and failing to keep the tremor out of her voice.

He slumped against the tunnel wall with a moan. Her arms encircled him, but his weight was too much, dragging them both to the cramped floor.

"Kit?" She spoke his name quietly, then shook him, yet still got no response. Panic crept into the darkness, pulsing through the air, until she saw things that weren't there, heard voices in the silence, and felt a presence other than her own and his.

"No," she said firmly, tightening her jaw and fighting the adrenaline rushing into her bloodstream. "No." She would not give into rampant confusion and the terror it would bring.

A vague sensation, like a touch, tugged at her sleeve, and she whirled around. *Back off, Jack*, she growled from some deep place in her mind. *He is mine. You cannot have him.*

She turned back to Kit. Using every grain of strength and every shred of will she had left, she hauled him to his feet, only to find her last inch of strength wasn't enough. He slipped back against the wall.

Breathing heavily, she rested her forehead on his and began to pray and curse in a litany of desperation, her hands wrapped around the collar of his tunic.

"Dear God . . . help me . . . help me get this stupid son of a bitch and two fathers to his feet . . . Excuse me, Melanie. No offense and nothing personal intended." She pulled him up and pressed her chest against his to hold him. "Damn you . . . Kit Carson, you better find whatever the hell it is you just lost, like your consciousness, or I'll drag you out of here by your feet. You hear that? Your feet. And on this floor that's going to be one poor way to go." She shoved her shoulder beneath his arm and felt her knees give way. She locked them, trapping herself into immobility. "Last chance, outlaw," she hissed between her teeth. "Come to, or suffer the consequences."

His knee bumped hers in a feeble, unfinished step, but it was enough.

Twelve

Kristine swirled around the dance floor on her father's arm, a vision in yards of white lace and satin. She was primped, coiffured, curled, powdered, and lipsticked to within an inch of her life. Rouge had been unnecessary; she glowed like a full-blown rose.

Across the room, her very own husband was waltzing with her mother. Muriel glowed a little herself, even if the man she danced with was not who she might have chosen for her daughter, a man wearing a white tunic lightly embroidered down the front in gold thread, a melange of anciently inscribed gold bracelets, and roan braid that hung below his shoulder blades. It was the biggest wedding her family had ever pulled off.

The Golden Plum, the finest caterer in northern Colorado, had plied the guests with champagne and strawberries, pricy treats of shrimp and lobster without a chicken breast or Swedish meatball in sight, and the tiniest little sandwiches Kristine had ever seen. The cake was four tiers of chocolate confection draped and laden with white frosting and candied violets to match her eyes. She and Kit had already vowed to eat themselves into indulgence and beyond on the leftovers.

They had a band, practically an orchestra. They'd rented the country club hall and had it decked to decadence in cascades of white carnations and lavender—to match her eyes. Up by the bandstand, an undeniably gaudy display had her and Kit's initials intertwined in pink rosebuds within a heart of baby iris—to match her eyes. Her bouquet was white roses, baby's breath, and orchids of a color to match her eyes.

This was her wedding, and Kristine knew she was only going to get two. She'd wanted to do this one with pomp and circumstance, and her father hadn't balked at the price.

Kit had insisted on buying all those flowers that matched her eyes, and she loved them, each and every one. She'd privately paid the caterer, but the band was her father's, all twenty pieces of it.

Jenny and her mother had taken over her dress and the bridesmaids' apparel with a vengeance. Denver had never seen such a burning commitment to shopping. The two older women had lost five pounds apiece, though Jenny swore she'd lost six.

"Mrs. Carson?"

Her father whirled her around and into her husband's arms.

"Yes, Mr. Carson?" She grinned up at him.

"I have married you twice, *patni*, once under the Eyes of Buddha, and once in the way decreed by your Christian Bible, though I doubt God had a hundred guests and four tiers of cake in mind as additions, and still you keep your secret from me. This is not the manner of a good wife." He arched one brow at her.

He had married her under the Eyes of Buddha, literally, in a monastery tucked into the highlands of the Forbidden Kingdom of Mustang, now a province of Nepal and once his home. A wizened lama with a sparse gray beard had given them their vows while Kit had lain on what she feared would be his deathbed.

She'd gotten him out of Chatren-Ma, but she'd never told him how. Looking at him now, with his skin returned to its normal healthy color and the energy of his life-force surrounding her, she knew she never would. To tell him was an invitation to disaster. He wanted to go back.

"You'll never get it out of me," she said, flashing him another smile. The secret was locked in her heart, and she'd learned how to keep her thoughts to herself.

In answer, he swung her up into his arms, his own grin turning sly. "I have a secret, also, Kreestine. One it would do you well to learn. Maybe we can trade, eh?"

He strode out of the ballroom with long sure strides, but Kristine barely noticed they were leaving.

He had a secret? From her? She doubted it. She'd spent two weeks in that monastery cooling his heated brow and talking to every monk not under a vow of silence. She'd learned plenty, some of which she could have done without.

The gold mask, for instance, had been a gift from an Asian princess in the throes of unrequited love. The semiprecious stones and the luxurious sheepskin spread on his bed had been the not-so-subtle offering of a wealthy Indian woman to the monastery. She'd wanted to "buy" herself a house-boy, and had chosen Kit from the ranks of novices not destined for a life of pure faith. He'd been fifteen. Kristine had figured the rest out on her own, and decided she would have run away too.

She'd found another of his secrets in his saddle-bags, and she'd laughed until the tears rolled down her face, a much-needed stress reliever that had left her sobbing in a huddle on the ground. She'd been so afraid he would die.

Days later, after his fever had broken, she'd found the humor again and wondered how the Turk was liking his new haircut.

"What secret?" she asked Kit now, her arms wrapped around his neck.

"A trade, nothing less." He set her back on her feet by their new car, a Cadillac of all things. He'd toured every showroom, then surprised her by opting for what he called an "American thoroughbred." Barbar-ian, indeed, she'd thought to herself. The man had impeccably refined taste. It had taken her all of two minutes to get used to traveling in style.

She looked around the parking lot. "We can't leave, Kit. It's our party."

"The secret, *patni*." He pressed against her and seared her with a kiss. Damn the man, she thought, he knew all her soft spots—his kisses and her curiosity.

"You first." She sighed the words along the line of his jaw, stealing more kisses on the way.

"You will have our child."

There he went again, stunning her into silence.

"Well—well yes," she stammered when she recovered. "Someday, no doubt, we'll have children and—"

"Nine months, Kreestine." His hand slid across her tummy. "In nine months you will have this child."

"Impossible," she gasped. "You can't know that."

"This I know, and more." He kissed her cheek.

"More?" She angled her head back to look up into eyes soft with mystery, and her voice lowered to an incredulous whisper. "You know if it's a boy or a girl?"

"Yes." A rogue's smile teased his mouth. "But for this knowledge there is a price."

"No." She forced herself to say no. She couldn't wouldn't. . . . pregnant? With his baby? Unconsciously she covered his hand with hers. "Make me a promise." She had to know.

"I will not return without you, I promise. I will prepare myself in a manner to lessen the effect of the cavern, I promise. There are ways. And I promise our . . . child, will only need one father to see him, or her, through life. All these things I promise."

She took a deep breath. He never broke a promise. "I think you've already realized that I must have found another way out of, and consequently into, Chatren-Ma."

"Yes."

"The only people who ever need to go back into the caverns again is a spelunking team, hopefully under the auspices of a certified historical and archaeological expedition."

"Yes," he agreed patiently. When she didn't continue, he prompted her. "The way, Kreestine?"

"Do you know how many cells are in the monastery?"

"About a hundred, not counting the shrines, meeting rooms, work areas, and kitchen," he answered, giving her a quizzical look.

"It's common sense, Kit," she said. "A hundred men, monks, without nary a woman to tote and clean for them, would not have hauled their water through that maze of paths, tunnels, and traps of emptiness day after day after day. They would have built something, like plumbing, or a viaduct, or at least a shortcut to the river."

His eyes widened. "You found a path to the river?"

"It used to be a path, now it's a rockslide."

"You destroyed a path to the river?"

"I was desperate, and at the time, and to this day, I'm very grateful we didn't go down with the rocks, though that might have been quicker than walking over them. Your turn." An expectant—very expectant—smile lit her face. She thought she was finished. He didn't.

"What is the location of the path inside the monastery?"

"Kit," she warned.

"Our child will probably lead such an expedition, *patni*. He should know these things."

"He?"

"A son," he confirmed with a smile, taking her back into his arms. "Our son."

She held him for all she was worth, brimming with happiness. Then she stretched up on tiptoe and whispered in his ear, "Ninth cell east of the granary on the north side."

The adventure of life with the outlaw Carson, it seemed, would never end.

THE EDITOR'S CORNER

Nothing could possibly put you in more of a carefree, summertime mood than the six LOVESWEPTs we have for you next month. Touching, tender, packed with emotion and wonderfully happy endings, our six upcoming romances are real treasures.

The first of these priceless stories is SARAH'S SIN by Tami Hoag, LOVESWEPT #480, a heart-grabbing tale that throbs with all the ecstasy and uncertainty of forbidden love. When hero Dr. Matt Thorne is injured, he finds himself recuperating in his sister's country inn—with a beautiful, untouched Amish woman as his nurse. Sarah Troyer's innocence and sweetness make the world seem suddenly new for this world-weary Romeo, and he woos her with his masterful bedside manner. The brash ladies' man with the bad-boy grin is Sarah's romantic fantasy come true, but there's a high price to pay for giving herself to one outside the Amish world. You'll cry and cheer for these two memorable characters as they risk everything for love. A marvelous LOVESWEPT from a very gifted author.

From our very own Iris Johansen comes a LOVESWEPT that will drive you wild with excitement—A TOUGH MAN TO TAME, #481. Hero Louis Benoit is a tiger of the financial world, and Mariana Sandell knows the danger of breaching the privacy of his lair to appear before him. Fate has sent her from Sedikhan, the glorious setting of many of Iris's previous books, to seek out Louis and make him a proposition. He's tempted, but more by the mysterious lady herself than her business offer. The secret terror in her eyes arouses his tender, protective instincts, and he vows to move heaven and earth to fend off danger . . . and keep her by his side. This grand love story will leave you breathless. Another keeper from Iris Johansen.

IN THE STILL OF THE NIGHT by Terry Lawrence, LOVESWEPT #482, proves beyond a doubt that nothing could be more romantic than a sultry southern evening. Attorney Brad Lavalier certainly finds it so, especially when he's stealing a hundred steamy kisses from Carolina Palmette. A heartbreaking scandal drove this proud beauty from her Louisiana hometown years before, and now she's back to settle her grandmother's affairs. Though she's stopped believing in the magic of love, working with devilishly sexy Brad awakens a long-denied hunger within her. And only he can slay the dragons of her past and melt her resistance to a searing attraction. Sizzling passion and deep emotion—an unbeatable combination for a marvelous read from Terry Lawrence.

Summer heat is warming you now, but your temperature will rise even higher with ever-popular Fayrene Preston's newest LOVESWEPT, FIRE WITHIN FIRE, #483. Meet powerful businessman Damien Averone, brooding, enigmatic—and burning with need for Ginnie Summers. This alluring woman bewitched him from the moment he saw her on the beach at sunrise, then stoked the flame of his desire with the entrancing music of her guitar on moonlit nights. Only sensual surrender will soothe his fiery ache for the elusive siren. But Ginnie knows the expectations that come with deep attachment, and Damien's demanding intensity is overwhelming. Together these tempestuous lovers create an inferno of passion that will sweep you away. Make sure you have a cool drink handy when you read this one because it is hot, hot, hot!

Please give a big and rousing welcome to brand-new author Cindy Gerard and her first LOVESWEPT—MAVERICK, #484, an explosive novel that will give you a charge. Hero Jesse Kincannon is one dynamite package of rugged masculinity, sex appeal, and renegade ways you can't resist. When he returns to the Flying K Ranch and fixes his smoldering gaze on Amanda Carter, he makes her his own, just as he did years before when she'd been the foreman's young daughter and he was the boss's son. Amanda owns half the ranch now, and Jesse's sudden reappearance is suspicious. However, his outlaw kisses soon convince her that he's after her heart. A riveting romance from one of our New Faces of '91! Don't miss this fabulous new author!

Guaranteed to brighten your day is SHARING SUNRISE by Judy Gill, LOVESWEPT #485. This utterly delightful story features a heroine who's determined to settle down with the only man she has ever wanted . . . except the dashing, virile object of her affection doesn't believe her love has staying power. Marian Crane can't deny that as a youth she was filled with wanderlust, but Rolph McKenzie must realize that now she's ready to commit herself for keeps. This handsome hunk is wary, but he gives her a job as his assistant at the marina—and soon discovers the delicious thrill of her womanly charms. Dare he believe that her eyes glitter not with excitement over faraway places but with promise of forever? You'll relish this delectable treat from Judy Gill.

And be sure to look for our FANFARE novels next month—three thrilling historicals with vastly different settings and times. Ask your bookseller for A LASTING FIRE by the bestselling author of THE MORGAN WOMEN, Beverly Byrne, IN THE SHADOW OF THE MOUNTAIN by the beloved Rosanne Bittner, and THE BONNIE BLUE by LOVESWEPT's own Joan Elliott Pickart.

Happy reading!

With every good wish,

Carolyn Nichols

Carolyn Nichols
Publisher, FANFARE and LOVESWEPT

NEW!
Handsome Book Covers Specially Designed To Fit Loveswept Books

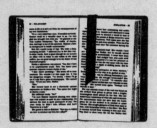

Our new French Calf Vinyl book covers come in a set of three great colors— royal blue, scarlet red and kachina green.

Each 7" × 9½" book cover has two deep vertical pockets, a handy sewn-in bookmark, and is soil and scratch resistant.

To order your set, use the form below.